A Turn in the Road

A Turn in
the Road

Jane McLoughlin

ROBERT HALE · LONDON

Typeset in 10/16 Baskerville by
Derek Doyle & Associates, Liverpool.
Printed in Great Britain by
St Edmundsbury Press, Bury St Edmunds, Suffolk.
Bound by Woolnough Bookbinding Limited.

1

Anna Turl wished that she had never come to this God-forsaken place. Not that she'd had much choice in the matter. Her boss at the travel agency, Nick Gold, said she must go and go she must. Nick, who owned the company, gave her this spiel about the trip being an honour for her, representing Golden Tours abroad and all that, and how being the current Golden Girl with her picture on all the advertising posters would open doors on a golden future for her and hers. As far as Nick was concerned, her and hers certainly didn't include Tom. It meant her and Nick. Nick never thought she was serious about Tom, anyway. He kept saying 'Anna Turl, Golden Girl' in a sing-song voice like a mantra. He thought it had a ring to it, but it just sounded silly to Anna.

She'd told him that once she and Tom were married, she'd be giving up work and living happily ever after as an assistant bank manager's wife. He'd laughed and said she was bound to change her mind, a girl like her, whatever that was meant to mean. She didn't argue. She was glad enough to earn the financial extras that went with being Nick's Golden Girl. Or she had been so far. This trip to a travel agents' confer-ence in a big hotel in Brittany was part of all that, and at the moment she was having serious second thoughts. But it was a bit late now, and so here she was in her ageing car, blinded by spray and buffeted in the slipstream of speeding lorries, on a dual carriageway taking her God knew where. She was completely lost. She didn't even know what time it was: she'd forgotten to wind her watch.

Worst of all, the car was faltering. It coughed, revived, then choked again. It was a sun-loving Italian model and did not like the all-pervading spray. And even if the car had been running well, she was scared stiff driving in these conditions. Her knuckles were white from gripping the wheel.

She saw the slip road just in time. She took it. She didn't know where it went, but then she had no idea where she was, anyway. At least she could see where she was going in spite of the rain.

It was almost dark. In the fading light this was a wind-crippled, empty landscape. The rain, driven over an open moor, fled across the road ahead like a galloping herd of terrified beasts. Anna didn't like it.

But there was a village: at least some dark cottages and a garage with one single light swinging back and forth over a row of old-fashioned, inefficient-looking petrol pumps. She stopped and sounded the car-horn. At last a light went on inside the dark building. A sulky teenage girl slouched towards her.

Anna said in French, 'What awful weather.' The girl seemed not to understand her accent.

'Fill it up?' she said, in a language that hardly seemed like French to Anna, who had a certificate of fluency in the language.

'Can you tell me if I'm on the right road for the Château de Goriac?' she asked. She spoke slowly in case the girl was a foreigner.

The girl, with both hands holding the pump nozzle, pointed ahead with her chin.

'Is it signposted?'

'There's nowhere else to go before you get there.'

'That's a relief,' Anna said. She handed over money for the petrol.

'Thirty kilometres or so. More, maybe,' the girl said, counting the money.

She was a sullen creature, about sixteen years old. But the village was completely desolate. The windows of most of the cottages were boarded. Anna thought she must get lonely, a young girl in a place like that.

Anna drove on for miles. She didn't seem to be getting anywhere. There wasn't a single light in view. There seemed to be nothing but open country without any sign of life. No wonder that girl at the garage was so withdrawn. She probably didn't speak to another real human being outside her own family from one week to the next.

Then the car choked; the engine died. The lights went out.

Anna tried to start it. It didn't even turn over. She turned the lights off, then back on. Nothing. Without the heater, the car was already growing cold.

She opened the window and tried to see through the rain. There must be some sign of people close by. All she could hear was the wind.

She didn't know what to do. Go for help? Better to stay in the car. At least it was dry. If she started to walk back to the garage or forward to the Château de Goriac she wouldn't be able to see where she was going. She might fall into a ditch, twist her ankle, die of hypothermia. No, it was better to stay where it was dry.

So she sat there. From time to time she tried to start the car. If something in the engine got wet it sometimes dried out after a while. But it gave no sign of life. Anna began to shiver. She could get out and fetch her suitcase from the boot to find something warm to wear, but if she got out of the car, she'd be drenched in seconds and then she'd be wet as well as cold. She was scared of opening the car door and getting out. The darkness out there seemed very unfriendly.

She cursed Nick Gold. This was all his fault. She'd never asked him to promote her as his stupid Golden Girl. Then she found herself blaming Tom. He should never have let her do this trip alone. He'd agreed to take the Eurostar on Friday and spend the weekend here with her; he could've taken a few more days leave from the bank and come with her.

She was being unfair, of course, she knew that. It wasn't Tom's fault:

it was just that she wished so much that he was with her. Nothing ever seemed so bad when Tom was there. Tom would never have allowed this to happen. He'd have had a spare set of whatever car part it was that had gone wrong, he'd know how to deal with it; and he wouldn't be afraid of the dark. Plus he'd have had a sleeping-bag in the back just in case. Prepared for anything, that was Tom. If only I'd listened, she thought.

But there was no point blaming herself now. She waited. There was nothing else to do. She wondered when she could start looking for signs of dawn. She thought, what does dawn look like, in a place like this? She'd seen in the dawn often enough, but always indoors and in a town. Would anyone at the hotel notice she hadn't arrived? How soon would they send out a search party?

Something touched the car. Anna cringed. There were muffled sounds like muttering. The car began to rock like a cradle. She tried to shout but it came out as a scared whisper. 'Who's there? Is anyone there?' There wasn't any answer but the muttering sound, and the movements didn't stop. Then there was a dry, old man's cough. Surely I'm not afraid of an old man, she told herself. She opened the car window and peered out into the darkness. Then she heard a definite 'baa'. Sheep, of course. They had barged into the unexpected obstacle of a car. She felt comforted. Someone must own the sheep. Someone was bound to check them in the morning.

But suddenly the sounds of the animals stopped. One bleated, then broke and ran. Others followed. That was what sheep did when they were frightened. She couldn't see them. She heard the patter of their feet on the road. Then there was only the sound of the wind and the rain. What had frightened them? Surely there couldn't still be real wild animals in Brittany, big cats, perhaps even wolves?

The wind sounded like film music. One of those black and white old-time chillers Tom liked. Dear Tom, he was of a different era. That was one of the things she'd liked about him when they met, he was such a straight, old-fashioned English gent, a man to rely on. She'd liked that about him, it was so different from what she was used to, which was the Nick Golds of this world. Anna had always liked older men. Of course there were a few things Tom was a bit straight-laced about, but she liked that, too. He had high standards and it boosted her self-esteem that he thought she was good enough for him, even if she was a few years younger. Thirteen years younger, to be exact. They both had to make allowances. She had been twenty-six when she met him, and that was nearly two years ago. It's not as if she were still a silly young girl; and he was only just middle-aged. But there were things he was better off not knowing about her, and vice versa. For instance, Anna had never let him meet her mother, and she never would, not if she could help it. She told him she lived in Birmingham, and they'd lost touch, and he believed her. If only, Anna thought. And it would've been better if he'd never let her meet his mama. Mrs Pritchard had disliked Anna on sight and never let Tom forget it. Anna could imagine what Tom's mother would say if she knew about this little episode, taking it for granted Anna was so feather-brained she must've run out of petrol or something daffy like that. At least there was one comfort: Mrs Pritchard wasn't here. Mrs Pritchard! Soon she herself would be the Mrs Pritchard who mattered. The present incumbent would be retired to the status of has-been.

Suddenly there was a new sound. It was the noise of an engine. There was a glow of light ahead growing larger and wider.

Anna opened the car door and ran into the rain in front of the oncoming vehicle, waving her arms and shouting. He must be able to see her. The vehicle was too big for a car, more like a pick-up truck. There was a squeal of brakes and it stopped. She ran to the driver's window.

She was babbling, she was so relieved. 'Am I glad to see you,' she said in English, and then remembered and corrected herself and said it in French.

9

The driver opened the door and got down. He left the engine running. The headlamps picked out Anna's car. She couldn't see his face.

'It died on me,' she said. 'It just stopped.'

Once again she spoke in English without thinking and then had to translate.

He walked to the car. With the light behind him he seemed huge. Then he turned back to her. His hat was pulled down tight against the rain and she still couldn't see his face.

'Open the bonnet,' he said. His accent was odd, but he spoke the sort of French she could understand.

Oh, thank God, she thought, he knows about cars. She sat in the driving seat with the door open and the rain coming in and waited while he leaned over the engine. Then he stepped back.

'There's nothing I can do here,' he said.

'Can you take me somewhere I can phone a garage?'

He wiped his hands on his trousers. He didn't seem to notice the water dripping from the brim of his hat and running down his face. He paid no attention to the rain.

He said, 'I'll give you a tow.'

He sounded tired. His accent was definitely odd. Perhaps he was drunk.

She said, 'You're very kind.'

He went back to his pick-up. He'd got a length of rope and went down on his knees on the wet road to attach the rope to her car. Then she heard him cough as he got a mouthful of exhaust when he fixed the other end underneath the truck.

She had never been towed before. He seemed to be going far too fast, but there was no way she could signal him to slow down. She tried to keep her eyes fixed on the pick-up's tail lights and steer as best she could, but they blurred in the rain. She thought the man was going the wrong way. He hadn't turned back to the village with the garage. She told herself she was being silly. He'd know somewhere closer.

It seemed ages before he turned off the road. In the side-sweep of his headlamps she saw a wooden box nailed to a post marked *Poste*, and then a sign *Privée* and under it *Entrée Interdit*. The car began to bounce over potholes. She found it hard to keep hold of the wheel, and she thought, perhaps he needs to be drunk to drive this track every time he goes out.

His headlamps showed a grey stone wall ahead and then a large stone farmhouse. Anna looked, expecting to see lights from the house, but it was in darkness. The pick-up stopped and her car slid to a halt.

The man got out holding a lighted storm lantern. He was like a figure in a woodcut. She could see his dark legs as he walked away and then he disappeared. She heard a heavy door open, then the light moved across straw stacked inside a barn. The man came back.

'We'll push your car into the barn there,' he said. 'Do you understand? Better out of the rain.' He made the motion of shoving with both arms extended.

When the car was under cover in the barn, he said, 'You have suitcase?'

Anna said, 'Oh, let's wait and see if the garage can send someone out at once.'

But the man opened the boot and took out her case. 'Change clothes maybe,' he said.

He talked as if his mouth wasn't used to going through the motions of speech.

'I don't want to be any trouble to your wife,' Anna said.

'No trouble,' he said.

Taking up the storm lantern and the case, he led the way to the house. A large dog ran out of the shadows.

'Boris,' the man shouted, and the dog flattened itself against the ground.

'He's obedient,' she said.

11

The man said nothing.

She thought he probably beat the dog, it looked so abject.

She could hear the regular throb of a motor.

'What's that?' she said. Perhaps he had a workshop here, a workshop with employees.

'Generator,' he said, 'for electricity.'

The house was cold. There was no sign of a woman there. The fire in the kitchen range at the far end of the grey stone-floored room had gone out. There was a sideboard and a big square table. The sink was full of dirty pans. There were no taps over the sink. A cast iron pump, its shaft disappearing through a hole in a rotting wooden cover in the floor beside the sink, appeared to supply the water. The place was like a museum, and everything was covered in thick dust. There was definitely no wife now and by the looks of it, there hadn't been one for years.

When the man took off his hat and waterproof coat, Anna saw him properly for the first time. He was not very tall, after all. She'd been fooled by the straight way he held himself. She wondered if he'd been a boxer when he was young; his face seemed a bit squashed, like pictures of old prizefighters. He had long dirty black hair and a straggling grey moustache.

Anna felt uneasy, but he didn't look particularly dangerous. He was watching her. Like any other young woman, she was used to men looking at her but this one seemed to be assessing her as if she were a beast at the market.

'I'd better try the garage,' she said.

'I do it,' he said. 'They don't speak English, they barely speak French. They're ignorant Bretons. Fit for nothing. They're shit, I tell you that.'

This sudden flare-up of hatred was a bit disconcerting, but then he smiled and said, 'Those wet clothes. You get dry.'

He took her suitcase and she followed him through a small lobby and

12

up a surprisingly narrow stone staircase to a long uncarpeted passage that seemed to run the length of the house. Their footsteps were loud on the bare boards. There was a musty smell and she had the feeling that anything she touched would strike cold and clammy. She tried to tell herself there was no reason to be frightened. It was absurd to think that there was something threatening about this cold, echoing house, and the surly man. This was how poor peasants in an area like this lived. These were the kinds of conditions that a developing tourist industry could improve. Nick Gold would be proud of her; she was learning from her experiences.

Her rescuer opened a door and showed her into a room. He didn't go in but leaned round the door jamb and turned on the light.

'You use this,' he said. He pointed to another door in the room. 'Bathroom,' he said, smiling with what she took to be pride at the facilities he could offer. She had a vision of him showing off a holiday let to a client.

She said, 'Thank you. My name is Anna Turl.'

He nodded, but he didn't say anything and then he left, closing the door behind him.

The room was surprising. It was clean, with an old-fashioned brass bed covered with a bright patchwork quilt. There were sentimental pictures of Victorian domestic scenes on the walls. By the window was a dressing-table with a gilt mirror. It was a woman's room, Anna decided, probably his daughter's, but not much used. She imagined the girl had left home and only came back on rare visits. She must dread those trips, if the clothes in the wardrobe were any clue to the sort of girl she was. They were cheap, too bright and flashy.

Anna went to the window to close the curtains. She wouldn't put money on her rescuer not being a bit of a peeping Tom. Behind the glass she could make out the rough grain of wood. There were shutters. They were closed. No wonder, with the tearing wind she could still hear outside.

There was a mark on the window sill. Crude letters had been cut into the wood. The carver had had trouble with curves, but she could read it. *Rosa Calvo*, and then a date, *11.4.98*.

She wondered who had done it. Perhaps it was the bored daughter. Reading those letters gave Anna a funny feeling. It was a night for ghosts. It was silly to be scared. After all, if the car had broken down in daylight, if there had been no wind and rain, she wouldn't have been frightened at all.

She changed into the warmest clothes she'd brought with her, a sweater and jeans. She'd packed for central heating in a luxury hotel, not an icy bedroom in a damp old house. She was also hungry. By the time the car was repaired and she got to the hotel, the kitchens would be closed. She hoped the old cliché was true and that all French peasants did eat like lords.

She turned the door handle. The door wouldn't open. She rattled it, pushing and pulling. Nothing happened.

She shouted, hoping the man could hear. There was no answer.

There was a keyhole in the door. She tried to look through it. There was a key in the lock: the door was locked from the outside.

At first Anna didn't believe it. Then she thought he'd turned the key without thinking and then got caught up in something he had to do, like feed his animals, and had forgotten her. She'd no idea what time it was, or what needed to be done for animals at that time of day, whatever it was. She even told herself it was after working hours and he was telephoning around trying to get someone out to mend her car. It was easier to tell herself that than to face the alternative.

In the end, though, two years of going out with Tom began to tell: she had to face facts. Sometimes she had to admit that if Tom was under pressure he sounded like someone reading from a manual on good management practice. But he was invariably right. She could almost hear his voice. 'Set out the facts; assess the situation; take appropriate action.'

14

She was imprisoned in an isolated farmhouse God knew where by a maniac. No, perhaps he wasn't a maniac. He could be an opportunist who thought there was something to be gained by keeping her there. He was obviously dirt poor, so perhaps he thought someone would pay a ransom for her. Perhaps the daughter whose room she was now occupying had run away and left him, and Anna reminded him of her.

There was no point in speculating. She couldn't assess the situation, and she couldn't act. She was completely helpless. She knew then what it felt like to be absolutely alone. No one was going to miss her at the hotel. They'd simply think she'd decided not to go to the conference after all and forgotten to cancel. None of the delegates would miss her, either. They didn't know her. When it came to checking registration, they'd think the girl from Golden Tours had changed her mind.

Worst of all, Tom wouldn't know she was missing. They'd agreed not to phone each other while she was away. She'd told him she preferred it that way because she didn't want the other delegates to think she wasn't totally professional and independent, but really it wasn't that. Tom would never ring her from work, and he wouldn't let either of them have mobile phones because he thought they caused brain tumours. So he made all his personal calls from home. And home for Tom meant his mother's house. He hadn't even got an extension in his bedroom. The telephone was in the hallway, and his mother could overhear every word he said. Anna hated talking to him knowing his mother was listening and they would talk about what she said afterwards. Tom's mother hated her. It wasn't just a question of her being afraid of losing her precious son to a young woman; Mrs Pritchard – and she never asked Anna to call her anything except Mrs Pritchard, even when she and Tom had got engaged – did not like her personally. Anna didn't like Mrs Pritchard, either, which made them quits, Anna thought. But this trip to Brittany was the first time she'd been away from Godlingford alone since she and Tom started going out, and she didn't want his mother turning her into the monosyllabic acquaintance she'd sound like knowing the old bitch was listening to their telephone conversation.

Thinking of all the people who wouldn't even notice she was missing, Anna began to feel really sorry for herself. Then the thought that Mrs Pritchard would definitely be pleased if she disappeared for good made her just angry enough to stop her crying, but she was very close to tears.

She heard the key in the lock. The door opened. The man stood watching her. She waited, not daring to move.

She asked, 'Have you found someone to mend the car?' She had some idea that if she pretended she didn't know he'd locked her in, he might think better of it and let her go.

There was something about the way he stood there in the doorway staring. It was as though he could not understand what she was saying.

'No telephone here,' he said. 'You stay here.'

'I can't stay here,' she said. 'People are expecting me. I have friends. They'll be worried if I don't get in touch.'

He continued to stare, saying nothing. Then he grabbed her arm and yanked it behind her back. He pushed her in front of him along the passage, down the stairs and into the kitchen. There was no way she could resist. It felt as though her arm was breaking.

Through the kitchen window she saw that it was morning. She could see across a yard to the barn where her car was hidden. A bird suddenly started to sing outside somewhere. A cock crowed.

The man pushed her down on a bench at the table. There was a chain on the table. It had a crudely-made clamp at one end. He took it up. Before she realized what he was doing, he'd put the clamp round her ankle and padlocked it.

'No,' she shouted. She kicked out at him, but the chain was so heavy she could scarcely lift her leg.

He didn't say anything, just went across the room and fastened the other end of the chain to a ring set low down in the wall.

Anna didn't dare speak. She watched him move around the kitchen,

16

preparing to go out. The dog was barking outside. The man went out, carrying a bucket.

She sat, feeling numb. What made it worse was the ordinary sounds around her in the echoing kitchen, the faint creak of the blackened stove as the hotplate cooled, the drip of water in the well, the sound of sparrows. It made her feel she was trapped in something permanent, that it was her life with Tom in Godlingford that was a dream from which she had now woken.

2

About four o'clock in the afternoon, the mountains sucked the last of the light out of the sky. Great stone slabs, primitive objects of devotion, loomed in the pale light. Tom had been driving since eight that morning. He drove over the crest of one more hill to reveal yet another stretch of brown and purple Breton moorland laid out ahead of him.

A few miles more and he saw the gates of the hotel. The Château de Goriac, a name out of an old horror movie, and it looked the part. He drove under the huge granite arch of the gatehouse and there was the château set low on the flanks of a hill which rose steeply behind the grey stone battlements and pointed turrets of the building. Great dark evergreen bushes round the walls flapped like tarpaulins in the wind. He thought, I'll have a drink, then get into a bath. But then he thought, what kind of way is that to greet the woman I love?

There were cars parked on the sweep of grey gravel in front of the entrance portico. Otherwise, there was nothing to show that this was not still some reclusive aristocrat's private refuge.

He felt the wind tug his hat as he got out of the car. He took his overnight bag off the back seat and looked up at the windows high in the granite wall, wondering if she was watching him. He smiled, looking up at the windows, just in case she was looking down on him. He had no doubts at all that she would be looking out for him. She would have missed him as much as he had missed her. More, perhaps, because he had work he enjoyed doing and it kept his mind off her absence. Anna didn't like her job much, and she hadn't wanted to make this trip. If he hadn't promised to meet her here so that they could spend the weekend together, Tom thought she would probably have refused to come. Tom hoped she didn't feel he'd put pressure on her about this. The truth was, they could do with the money. Property wasn't getting any cheaper, and they were having quite a struggle to raise the deposit for a suitable place. Once they'd done that, she could tell Nick Gold and his job to go to hell.

In the meantime, they could make the best of it. And this weekend promised to be the very best.

There was an open log fire in the panelled foyer, stuffed animal heads on the walls. It could almost be Scotland, Tom thought happily.

The young woman behind the desk looked up and smiled at the big Englishman in the ridiculous tweed hat.

'It's a wild day,' she said in English. 'Can I help?'

He removed the hat and wondered for a moment how she knew he was English. He found her strong Breton accent difficult to follow.

'My name is Pritchard, Tom Pritchard,' he said speaking more slowly and clearly than usual, twiddling the brim of his hat with his fingertips. 'I'm meeting Miss Turl.'

The girl tapped at a computer keyboard.

'Miss Turl, did you say? There's no Miss Turl staying here.'

'Yes, Anna Turl. She's been here all week, with the travel agents' conference. Perhaps you have her booked under her company, Golden Tours, Holidays By Design, of Godlingford, Surrey.' When he said the full name of the firm it sounded ridiculous.

The girl tapped the keyboard again. She frowned. 'Miss Turl?' she said 'She was booked in from last Friday.'

'Yes,' Tom said 'last Friday night for two weeks.' He could hear his voice sounding very English, sounding like the sort of Englishman he didn't particularly admire.

'We expected her,' the girl said. 'The room was booked, but she never turned up. She never arrived.'

'Of course she did,' Tom said. 'She's been at the travel agents' conference all week.'

'No, sir. The room was pre-paid. Of course we kept it open, but she didn't arrive.'

'What do you mean?' Tom looked around as though checking that the girl had not hidden Anna somewhere in the foyer. 'She must've been in touch. She must have rung to say she'd broken down in her car, or something.'

The girl shook her head. 'We never heard from Miss Turl.'

'But I've come to spend the weekend with her,' Tom said. 'We're going off sightseeing for a few days. I've got time off from the bank. I'm the assistant manager.'

He saw the young woman looking at him. It seemed to him he was watching this happening to someone else. He realized the absurdity of what this other person who was not him had just said, as though an assistant bank manager's girl was immune from disappearance.

He said, 'She must be here somewhere. There must be someone who knows something about why she didn't turn up.'

'I'm sorry, sir, the people on the course all left early this afternoon for the weekend. They are going, some of them, to Nantes, others to Quiberon. They'll be back for Monday morning.'

'But if Anna didn't turn up, they must have said something? They must have checked?'

The girl shrugged. 'There are always a few who don't make it. They book and then they can't get away. There's a crisis at home. They think it doesn't matter if they change their minds, specially when it's a big company thing with the firm paying. They think they won't be missed. The delegates don't know each other before they arrive, isn't that so?'

'But she's been away all week, for God's sake,' Tom said. 'Where the hell is she if she's not here?'

'I'm very sorry, sir,' the girl said. She began to sound bored with repeating herself. 'If I were you, I'd check if she's at home. There's a public telephone across by the lifts.'

Tom looked around as though he hoped he might be in the wrong place. It was impossible that Anna would not have rung to let him know if something had happened to her. They'd agreed she wouldn't ring while she was away. He hadn't argued about that, although he knew she insisted on it because for some reason she wanted to give the impression she wasn't the sort of person who had domestic ties. She did that to please Nick Gold; Gold thought dedicated career women made the company look more professional. Surely, though, if something had happened, someone would have told him by now.

Tom put his tweed hat back on his head, as though it were a signal for action.

'No,' he said. 'I know she's not at home. Something terrible must have happened to her. Please call the police.'

The girl was startled. She thought she had misheard him.

'Call the police,' he said again.

3

'You did not speak with Mademoiselle Turl on the telephone at all during the week?' the policeman asked again. It seemed to Tom that he had been sitting in the police station all night answering the same question.

'She didn't want me to call.'

'You had a fight?'

'No, no fight.'

'A tiff? A small quarrel?'

'Nothing like that,' Tom said. 'She thought she wouldn't look like a serious businesswoman if her boyfriend was telephoning every five minutes. Her boss prefers it that way.'

'Her boss? Ah, yes, that is Mr Gold, is it not?'

'He'd promoted Anna to be his Golden Girl.'

The policeman lifted an eyebrow in a way Tom thought Frenchmen only did in British films. Tom realized how a literal translation of Golden Girl might look. 'That's an advertising thing,' he said. 'They had a poster campaign featuring Anna as the face of Golden Tours.'

The policeman pursed his lips. 'Not one telephone call in all of the week? Do you think perhaps she had no intention of going to the château, perhaps not to France at all?'

'Why should she do that?'

'Women do. Also men. They do not go where they are expected. They go somewhere else.'

'With someone else, you mean?'

'It could come to that.'

'Not Anna. Anna isn't like that at all. Please, you will look? You'll start a hunt.'

'A hunt?'

'A search.'

'Most certainly. But our resources are small. Goriac is not a large town. There is the question of where we start to search.'

Tom left the police station. It was very dark, except when the moon came out from behind the clouds. The town was deserted, the shops shuttered for the night. Goriac was some five kilometres beyond the château. It was a charming spot. The tourist brochures all said so. But Tom didn't notice the charm. He walked down a street of moonlit, warm, golden stone buildings with wrought-iron balconies and very French-looking shutters, and he didn't see any of it. He stood for a moment on the ancient bridge, looking down on a dark, fast-flowing, rock-strewn river, and he swore under his breath thinking of the mentality of the French police. They were dull, obstructive and completely unsympathetic.

He tried telling himself that Anna might not be lying dead in a ditch somewhere. He thought, maybe she has run off with some other man, as that Frog cop suspects. After all, she's twenty-seven years old and good-looking and I'm heading for forty and a bit of a bore. Let's face it, the high point in my life before I met her was playing rugby twice for Surrey. That's not going to mean much to a girl like Anna.

Tom decided that he needed a drink and he needed it quickly. He couldn't wait until he got back to the château. He walked across the bridge into a bar looking out on a small square. There was nobody behind the bar. Did nothing and no one in this place do any work? 'Hey, service!' he shouted in a voice that he recognized as an echo of the

24

imperialist holler of the Englishman among the primitive horde. At once he was embarrassed. As the barman approached, Tom muttered, 'Oh, sorry, *pardonnez-moi, monsieur*.' That was the extent of his French.

There was a man leaning on the counter beside him. Tom hadn't noticed him at first when he came in. He was an elderly Frenchman, smoking a Gitane, watching the smoke drift towards the ceiling. He turned and stared at Tom.

'You're English,' he said. 'I lived in London many years ago. You will join me in a drink?'

'I'll have the same as you,' Tom said.

'Two cognacs,' the man said.

When the drinks came the Frenchman said, 'Cheers' and then held out his hand. 'Alain Dulac,' he said, and smiled. 'I have been fishing all day and caught nothing.' Tom saw the fishing rod in the corner. 'But you,' the fisherman said, 'you look like a man who has the weight of the world on his shoulders.'

Tom took a deep breath. This was what he'd been looking for, a sympathetic ear. This man spoke good English. He had lived in England. He would understand. That French cop hadn't grasped anything he said. 'I've been with the police,' he said.

He told the fisherman the story.

'What do the police say about that?' Dulac asked. Tom saw he was one of those tall, thin, outdoor types with a weather-beaten face, a father figure in an old tweed coat who looked full of sympathy and rustic worldly-wisdom. He listened to Tom, a tall stooped old man, watching him through slightly bloodshot pale-blue eyes behind wire-framed spectacles. He was shabby, Tom saw, the elbows of his coat were patched and his corduroy trousers were rubbed at the knees.

'Either I murdered her,' Tom said, 'or she never left England. They assume she has run off with someone else. They say if her car broke down and she wandered off and got lost, or she'd fallen and hurt herself, they'd at least have found her car. And they haven't. Found her car, I mean.'

25

'Not necessarily,' Dulac said. 'After all, they haven't been looking for it, not until now. It's easy to get lost in a place like this and stay lost until someone starts looking for you. And the French policeman is not quick on the uptake. Inspector Baubel is my good friend, but he is not quick on the uptake.'

'They seemed more interested in grilling me about what happened before she left England than in finding her.'

'Ah, well,' Dulac said, 'they have to start somewhere.'

'But they're wasting time. What about search parties and looking for witnesses?'

'It's the middle of the night. And they don't know where to look. There's hundreds of kilometres between here and London and they can't even be sure she left England. They can check if her ticket was used, perhaps, but not till the morning. There are such things as office hours, my friend, here as well as London.'

'Surrey,' Tom said. 'Not London. Godlingford's in Surrey. They kept asking how we were getting on together. We love each other, for God's sake. We were going to get married. We *are* going to get married. It's all so stupid.'

'They have to look at all the possibilities, my friend. Women do run off.'

'But not Anna. Anna's not like that. Something's happened to her, and what could've happened that isn't bad, you tell me?'

'She could have lost her memory,' Dulac said.

'But surely someone would have found her by now. If you found someone who'd lost her memory, you'd tell the police. Wouldn't you?'

There was a short silence. Dulac signalled the barman to fill their glasses.

Tom drank, then said, 'I don't know what to do. I can't get over how people are about this. No one takes me seriously. First the girl at the château, then the police. You're the first person who's said a kind word to me. Are you a tourist?'

'I'm local. I do a bit of work around the hotels in the season when there's guests who want to walk off the beaten track. There's good trout fishing here, like in England. And the salmon here are as good as in Scotland. I know Britain. I was three years living there.'

Tom wasn't listening. He said, 'I can't believe it, they think I've murdered her.'

'What did she say when she left home?' Dulac asked.

'The last time I saw her she said she'd see me next week, which is today.' And then Tom suddenly announced, 'We don't live together.'

Tom was vaguely aware that he had embarrassed Dulac. He could tell that the Frenchman thought he was too old to blurt out things like that about his relationship with a woman. He'd sounded like a child. Dulac must wonder what kind of girl would be with such an old young man. Tom thought, I probably seem the kind of Englishman that a real little gold-digger might easily get her claws into, but then, being a typical Frenchman, looking at me with my pale, round, English face and short hair, body on the point of running to fat, he'll think she must be someone just like me, the sort of girl who gets her thrills choosing curtains and carpets, and talks about baby clothes and kitchen units. Are there still English girls like that?

Tom opened his wallet and showed a photograph of Anna. She was sitting on a patch of worn grass in Godlingford Municipal Park in front of a battalion of tulips. The setting wasn't much but Anna looked very pretty.

'What's a sexy girl like that doing with a fellow like you?' Dulac asked. It was a serious question. The police would want an answer before they would treat this case as anything but a broken romance. Dulac tried to make a joke of it, in case Tom had seen from his face what his true feelings were.

Tom looked at the photo. Anna was sexy: there was no mistake about it, but it was almost as if he hadn't noticed it before.

'The worst thing is,' Tom said, 'I've got to leave the day after tomor-

27

row to be back at work on Tuesday morning. I was going to spend all day with her on Sunday and catch the ferry back on Monday.'

The two cognacs he had drunk had gone to his head, but it was clear to him what Dulac was thinking, that with a girl like that, anybody else would quit his job to search until he found her.

'The bank won't like her going missing,' Tom said.

'I don't suppose she does either,' Dulac said.

'Of course,' Tom said, 'I only meant . . . it's so worrying.'

Tom sympathized with what he knew Dulac must think of him – a *petit bourgeois* banker worried what his boss might think! He hoped the English girl had gone off with a young Frenchman who would give her something to remember when she was back home buying curtains in Surrey. That's all right for someone like Dulac, Tom thought, it's Anna and my whole life we're talking about, not a story in a tabloid newspaper.

'But don't you worry,' Tom said, 'I'll keep tabs on the police here. I'm going to be keeping them up to the mark.'

Tom raised his hand in a farewell salute and marched out of the bar.

Back at the château he lay in bed in a room hung with shadowy tapestries, tormented by the sound of an accordion from a dinner dance in the hotel dining-room. The music had a relentless beat. He kept thinking of the policeman's voice at the station. 'Is there any evidence the lady ever reached this side of the Channel?'

Tom knew the policeman had put Anna down as a woman who had done a runner with her lover, a younger lover. He'd looked at Tom as much as to say, 'And who can blame her, a good-looking young girl like that? Why would she want to lumber herself with a middle-aged man like you?' The fisherman in the bar had also looked at him that way after he'd seen Anna's photo.

No, Tom thought, I wouldn't blame her. But she didn't do it. The power of suggestion might be strong, but Anna wouldn't let me drive hundreds of miles to find she'd gone off with someone else. She might be young and a little thoughtless, but she'd never be deliberately cruel.

Oh God, he said to himself, let me know. Let her be found. Let them find some sign that she did come here, that she didn't betray me. 'God, did I really think that?' he said aloud. 'What's happening to me?'

4

Inspector Parrish stood at the window of his second floor office in the ugly sixties block that was Godlingford Police Station. In the High Street below, he was watching Tom Pritchard. The man was obviously still in a temper. He had left Parrish's office in an angry mood. The policeman saw him push his way through the crowd. Someone had told him that Pritchard had once played rugby for the county. Rugby was as bad as soccer these days. Football had a lot to answer for. In Inspector Parrish's opinion, bad temper and a lack of manners was at the root of a lot of crime. Pritchard's squared shoulders, the clamped jaw and short clipped hair, all advertised aggression. Perhaps, Inspector Parrish thought, I shouldn't actually have come out with the suggestion that a beautiful twenty-something girl might possibly have had second thoughts about marrying a forty-year-old man and she'd run off and left him. But what else was I to say? The situation seemed obvious.

'Not a happy man,' Inspector Parrish said. 'Oh, not at all happy.'

He spoke to Sergeant Dicks seated at the second desk crammed into the little room. Dicks looked up. He was filling in a report of a recent break-in, trying to remember details he'd told himself at the time that he'd write up as soon as he got back to his desk, but of course he'd never had the time.

'What's that?' Dicks asked.

31

Inspector Parrish gave one last look out of the window.

'Nothing,' he said. 'I was just thinking that poor Mr Pritchard thinks we're not trying to find his vanishing girlfriend, but every time he comes in here he makes me more convinced that she must have run off and left him. How could a pretty girl, any girl, stay with a bloke like that?'

'He's all right,' Sergeant Dicks said. 'He's upset.'

He returned to his report. In his view Inspector Parrish, who had been divorced twice and now lived in what Dicks saw as a comic situation with a woman older than himself, a woman well over forty, if not fifty, was not a man in a position to pontificate on relationships. If Sergeant Dick's girl had disappeared when she was supposed to be at a business conference he would go mad too if the police suggested she might have staged her own disappearance to be with another man. Sergeant Dicks felt sorry for Mr Pritchard, who had been very helpful when he and his girl had gone into the bank to discuss a mortgage on a house. Sergeant Dicks was sorry for Mr Pritchard not only because Anna Turl had disappeared, but also because she was the sort of girl she obviously was. In the long run, Mr Pritchard would probably be better off without her, but that wasn't going to cut much ice with him at the moment. Sergeant Dicks thanked God his girl wasn't that sort. But Mr Pritchard's girl was very good-looking. In the photographs now scattered on Inspector Parrish's desk, he could see how good-looking she was. But she had that sexy look in her eyes and Sergeant Dicks thought a man would have to watch out for a girl with eyes like that. His own girl had short sight and wore glasses. Her eyes didn't come into it much.

Inspector Parrish said, 'You don't think, do you, that the man protests too much? That he might have done away with her himself?'

'Is he the type?' Dicks asked.

'What's the type?' Parrish asked. 'You didn't find anything incriminating when you searched her house?'

'Nothing at all. And we didn't find anything at his place either.

Nothing at all. He lives with his mother. He's not going to murder a girl in his mother's house, is he?'

'Maybe his mother's in on it,' Inspector Parrish said. 'Maybe she didn't like the girl and killed her, and he's putting on an act to cover up for her.'

Dicks didn't know what to say so he smiled.

'And what about the key?' Parrish asked. 'He said he didn't have a key.'

'What key?'

'To the girl's house. He'd have a key. He said he didn't but he must be lying. Of course he'd have a key to her place.'

'Why should he lie about it?' Sergeant Dicks asked.

'Exactly, why should he, when it's a perfectly ordinary thing for him to have a key to his fiancée's place?' Then Inspector Parrish said, 'Have you seen the mother?'

'Whose mother?'

'Her mother? The girl's mother.'

'Mrs Turl? I've seen her.'

'What did you think?'

'I don't know. I don't know what to think.'

Sergeant Dicks had seen Mrs Turl, and he had been genuinely shocked. It was the way she'd talked about her daughter. She had practically called her a slut. Mrs Turl wasn't worried about the girl. She assumed, like Inspector Parrish, that she had grown bored with a forty-year-old assistant bank manager and run off with a man her own age for a bit of fun. Sergeant Dicks had checked with some of Anna Turl's friends and they'd assumed the same thing; also Nick Gold, her boss at work at the travel agency, was angry about her skipping out on the business conference she was supposed to have attended. Nick Gold, who was young and trendy himself, with his gold ear-ring, said he knew Anna was a girl who liked a good time but he thought at least this time she'd put business first, knowing it was important. Gold had showed

33

Dicks a travel poster with a photo of Anna Turl on it. She was terrific-looking, dark, with a terrific tan and a wide and wonderful smile, and even as a picture she was sexy as hell. Sergeant Dicks might have settled on a homely kind of girl for himself, but he still knew a sex goddess when he saw one. It was obvious to Sergeant Dicks that Tom Pritchard didn't know exactly what kind of girl Anna was. Sergeant Dicks could tell by the way he acted, unless he was a fantastic actor, that he was a complete innocent about the sort of girl he was involved with. Sergeant Dicks wouldn't call her a slut, she was just a normal modern young woman who was perhaps a bit too good-looking and had those sexy eyes. But Sergeant Dicks believed in love, and he thought that a girl like Anna Turl who could have her pick of young men must really love Tom Pritchard. He couldn't see any other reason for her to choose him. Dicks was also a man of the world and he could see that Miss Turl might well have things in her past she'd rather conceal from an old-fashioned type like Pritchard.

'These girls,' Inspector Parrish said, 'they go missing and it gets reported to the police, it gets into the newspapers, and all sorts of things they thought they'd kept secret come out about them. Then they show up, they'd just gone off for a bit of fun, but while they were away people have found out these things girls like that never wanted anyone to know.'

Inspector Parrish's cynicism annoyed Sergeant Dicks.

'We haven't found out anything about Anna Turl,' Dicks said.

'Not yet we haven't,' Inspector Parrish said. 'But I'll put money on it that I'm right. Do you want to bet against it?'

'No,' Sergeant Dicks said sadly. 'I wouldn't put money on it. I'm just trying to keep an open mind, that's all.'

'An open mind is the best thing to have with a girl like that,' Inspector Parrish said.

34

5

Anna thought, this man isn't a maniac, he's a monster. At least if he was a maniac I could tell myself I'd been in the wrong place at the wrong time, he couldn't help himself. But it's not like that. He's doing this to me personally. I don't know why, but if it had been someone else he'd found broken down on the road, nothing would've happened. There was something about me which made him do this. Anyone who doesn't see it makes much difference doesn't understand what it's like to be in a situation like this. It does make a difference. I'm not simply a victim; I'm *his* victim. In a horrible way I can't begin to explain, it creates a relationship between us.

She blamed herself that she didn't realize at first that the man was a pervert. She thought he had grabbed the chance to kidnap her when it presented itself, and he'd demand a ransom. She was a bit surprised that he didn't ask about Tom, or Nick Gold, or her mother, who might be willing to pay to have her restored to them, but he didn't. Then she presumed he was waiting for a hue and cry to start about her going missing. He went out each morning and he usually brought a newspaper with him when he returned. Anna was glad about that. It meant that somewhere not far away real life carried on regardless. She might be chained in the kitchen each day, but there were ordinary people out there. As long as that was so, she could hope to be found and rescued.

She got through the days thinking that. She almost looked forward to being left alone each morning. Sitting in chains all day was nothing to what happened at night. At night, she didn't just want to escape: she wanted to pass out and never wake up.

The first night he came to her she thought he was going to rape her. He tied her wrists to the bedhead in the girlie room she thought had been his daughter's and he peeled off her clothes as though he was skinning a rabbit. Then he dropped his trousers and threw himself on top of her.

She told herself, I'd always thought that rape must be the worst thing for a woman, but I swear I'd rather he'd raped me. He couldn't. He couldn't get it up.

He ground his fist into her vagina; he gripped her breasts, tearing at her nipples; he bit her clitoris, chewing her like a cannibal about to eat her raw. Nothing worked. Then he smothered her face in his musty groin, panting, forcing his heavy, lumpen penis into her mouth and working her head up and down in a grotesque cunnilingus lubricated with blood.

She begged him to stop. She sobbed and pleaded. When she realized that he liked to hear her suffering like that, she tried not to give him the satisfaction, but it was impossible. It was too horrible to dwell on.

No wonder then, that the chain in the kitchen was a relief. At least she was alone. She'd never known anything like the silence of the place. That was frightening enough in itself. Maybe the sounds she was used to, of traffic and people shouting in the street and the men from the Gas Board digging up the road, weren't exactly natural, but those were the background noises that made her feel secure.

The kitchen had a malevolent atmosphere, too. It was full of dark shadows where the light never penetrated through the murky window. Even when there was a fire in the stove the place was never warm. At first she sat there, beyond thinking even, as the days ticked by towards the dreaded night. She passed the time in something like a trance, broken only by the pain where the metal shackle padlocked round her ankle had rubbed her skin raw. The chain, bolted to the ring low down on the kitchen wall, had 168 links, She'd counted them. Forty-two links to a metre. She could walk thirteen paces, back and forth. But she didn't.

At that stage she didn't hate him, even. She was too afraid of him.

She'd lost count of days. Sometimes it was light and mostly it was dark, that's all.

There was a newspaper lying on the kitchen table. She didn't know how long it had been there. Suddenly she noticed it.

There was a small photo of her on the front page. It was a photo Tom took soon after they met. She felt dizzy and the blood pounded in her ears.

It was difficult reading because her hands were trembling and something kept blurring her vision and she didn't know what it could be until she realized it was tears.

Police have scaled down the search for missing British travel agent Mlle Anna Turl, who failed to arrive for a conference at the new luxury Château de Goriac Hotel and Business Centre. Inspector of Goriac Police, M. Herbert Baubel, who is leading the inquiry, said last night that there was no evidence that Mlle Turl was ever in the area. No trace has been found of her red Fiat Panda car. M. Baubel added that the British police are now considering the possibility that she may never have intended to come to Brittany.

M. Baubel informed the Soir Express *that he has asked members of the local community to be vigilant, especially ramblers and hunters.*

M. Alain Dulac, an experienced local guide and prominent fisherman, told our reporter that the area where Mlle Turl is alleged to have disappeared is isolated and wild, but not hazardous to walkers or sportsmen who are properly equipped. He warned anyone who broke down or got lost not to try to go for help but to stay in their car. 'It is easier to find a car than a person who has fallen in the rocks or on the moors', he said.

Anna could read between the lines. She thought, they think I've run off with another man. But Tom will never let them get away with that.

37

Oh, my God, surely he wouldn't believe it. Perhaps he would, though. He always said it was a miracle that someone like me could really care for him. That awful mother of his had made him very unsure of himself with women. But we'd been through all that. He knows I love him. He can't help but know, I don't try to hide it. He's my life and my future and I love him. It's as simple as that. He doesn't even have to take it on trust. If the banker in him needed proof, he could see what I got out of it. No more bosses like Nick Gold; no more boring work earning my living; no more insecurity. He can give me what I want. And on top of all that, our sex life is great. When we first got it together that way, he seemed to be a bit startled by how enthusiastic I was about him physically. He couldn't quite believe how much I fancied him. But then because of the horrendous Mrs Pritchard the man was practically a virgin. It didn't take him long to catch up, though. We were happy together, for God's sake. No, Tom couldn't believe I'd leave him, whatever some cynical bloody policemen might tell him.

Reading the newspaper story was a jolt. Anna didn't know if she'd been expecting that if she simply waited long enough someone was bound to rescue her. Suddenly seeing the report in black and white made her see that that wasn't going to happen. She was on her own. She couldn't even be sure that Tom, too, hadn't given up on her and begun to concentrate on grieving and getting over her. There was nothing she could do to help him. She couldn't even help herself.

The words echoed in her head and became a question. Can I help myself? How can I help myself?

It brought her back to life. That evening she asked the man, 'Why are you keeping me here, Monsieur Calvo?' Her voice sounded cracked, feeble from lack of use.

He turned from the kitchen range where he was stoking the fire. He was furious.

'Where did you hear that name?' he asked. 'That is not my name.'

She didn't say anything. She had a terrible premonition that she

38

wasn't this man's first victim. Calvo was the name on the windowsill in the bedroom, Rosa Calvo. Perhaps she wasn't his daughter. But if she wasn't, who was she? It wasn't a French name. Was she another foreign tourist? Did Rosa Calvo die here . . . leaving only her name cut into the window frame? Were those Rosa Calvo's clothes hanging in the wardrobe? They were the clothes of a young woman. What had happened to her?

The man said, 'My name is Rostov.'

That wasn't a French name, either. It explained the weird way he spoke as though half his tongue were missing.

'The scum here call me Quimper because when I came here I was on the road to a town called Quimper. 'Quimper, Quimper?' I asked them. They all laughed. They're an ignorant bunch, the Bretons.'

He sounded very bitter. But he seemed willing to answer questions. Actually, it wasn't a question of being willing. It was as though he answered like Pavlov's dog, as though answering was the natural consequence of being asked.

Anna played a hunch. 'Where are you from?' She felt she was taking her first step towards helping herself. She looked at him and nearly lost her nerve. Then she told herself, why not? Knowledge is power.

He scowled. 'What do you want to know for? It won't do you any good,' he said. He seemed to be surprised at the sound of his own voice, as though he hadn't heard it in a long time.

He sat down at the table. His dark eyes were clouded over, as though they were looking inside his head at not very pleasant memories of the past.

'I am from the Ukraine,' he said. 'I took up with the Frenchwoman who had this farm. But the French treated me as an enemy. We learned to live apart from them, she and I.'

So once he had done something human like living with a woman.

'She died,' he said. 'She wasn't a young woman.'

'Who was Rosa Calvo?' Anna asked.

Quimper shrugged. She waited for him to speak but he said nothing. She could hear rain driving against the black glass of the uncurtained window.

There was a face at the window. She saw the momentary flash of it pressed to the glass. Then it disappeared.

She jumped to her feet.

'He saw me,' she shouted at Quimper. 'They've come for me.'

But Quimper had not moved. Slowly she took in how unconcerned he was. Then he got up and lighted the storm lantern, putting it on the table where the light flickered blue and orange on the grimy white walls.

The back door opened. Anna heard shuffling.

She cried out, 'In here. I'm in here.'

The silhouette of a man appeared in the doorway.

'Come on in, Toto,' Quimper said. 'You'll be hungry. I expected you before this. This is Toto,' Quimper said to Anna. 'He's come home.'

The newcomer stepped into the light. He was almost good-looking, about twenty. He had thick, curly red hair hanging down to his shoulders. He was carrying a canvas bag. He dumped it down on the table. It smelled of fish.

He stared at Anna. Then he smiled, showing broken teeth. He said something to Quimper, making an obscene gesture. Oh, God, Anna thought, please, not that.

6

Anna's mother was the one person who was bound to be feeling as badly about her disappearance as he was himself, Tom Pritchard thought. He had to talk to her. He knew Anna had not been in touch with her recently, but the police had told him that the old lady lived in Godlingford now. He thought it was time they met.

Mrs Turl's house was on a small estate built in the eighties, mock-Tudor, with diamond-paned windows and a studded front door inappropriately panelled with frosted glass.

Tom rang the bell. The opening bars of 'Land of Hope and Glory' startled him. He waited. He could hear sounds inside. Nothing happened. He didn't dare risk that door-bell cacophony again and knocked on the frosted glass.

'I'm coming, I'm coming,' he heard a woman call.

He assumed that the young woman who answered the door was some kind of nurse companion. Tom was startled at this young woman's appearance. She didn't look the caring type. She wore a black leather skirt that looked expensive and a baggy black sweater. She had a halo of blonde hair. He wondered if he had come to the wrong house.

'I'm looking for Mrs Turl,' he said.

'Yes,' she said. 'I'm Mrs Turl.'

Tom didn't know what to say. He'd got the impression from Anna

41

that her mother was a frail old lady. That wasn't strictly true; Anna hadn't given him any impression at all of her mother. But Tom's own mother was close to seventy, and it had never occurred to Tom that his future mother-in-law wouldn't at least be the same generation as his parent. When he looked closely, though, he could see the resemblance to Anna in the chiselled features. He supposed that if this woman's hair were not bleached she would be dark like Anna and there would be a strong family resemblance. Only they would look like sisters rather than mother and daughter. She's only a year or two older than I am, Tom thought, and she looks younger. Tom, with a mixture of disgust and curiosity, thought that people who saw them together would think that *she* was his girlfriend.

'Well?' Mrs Turl asked.

He could tell she thought he was selling something. 'I'm Tom Pritchard,' he said, trying to keep from looking at how young she was.

She looked at him as though appraising him and finding him wanting.

'You'd better come in,' she said.

Inside was like a show house. There were none of the touches of family life that Tom was used to in a home, even a well- ordered house like his mother's. Tom wondered if she'd bought the show house, lock, stock and barrel.

'Of course,' she said, 'you're the bank manager.'

She spoke in an offhand drawl which made her sound as if she already knew all about him, as if she'd had a secret report on him and there was very little he could say in his own defence.

'Assistant bank manager,' he said.

'Oh, yes,' she said. 'Anna's bloke.' She sat in the chair with her hands folded in her lap. She looked very calm with her back held straight, in her black clothes and the mass of blonde hair she was calm like a television interviewer about to talk to someone who might not be calm.

There were newspaper clippings piled on the sofa in the living-room.

Two of them had fallen on a pink rose on the patterned carpet and she bent over and picked them up. Tom could see they were stories from the papers reporting Anna's disappearance.

'I had someone here this morning to talk about Anna,' she said, 'and I got these out to show her.'

'Someone wanting to talk about Anna?'

'Yes, a young woman from one of the newspapers,' Mrs Turl said. 'She wanted to know about Anna, they want to do all they can to help. I let her have some old photos. The more people know what Anna looks like the better, don't you think?'

'I suppose so,' Tom said. 'I don't suppose it can do any harm, anyway. Which paper was she from?'

Mrs Turl shrugged. 'I can't remember now. They've got a readership of millions. She kept telling me that. She was very proud of it.' Mrs Turl smiled and it was Anna's smile.

'I've stopped reading them,' Tom said. 'It's always the same old speculation. There's never any new information.'

'I suppose they do what they can with what they've got,' Mrs Turl said. 'Well, this is a surprise.' She sat down by the mock-log fireplace and crossed her well-shaped legs. It occurred to Tom that if they put a picture of her in the paper, she wouldn't look like a grief-stricken mother.

'I didn't see much of Anna over the last few years,' she said.

Tom wished he hadn't come. He couldn't talk to this woman about his Anna. 'I suppose she didn't get to Birmingham that often,' he said. 'When did you move down?'

'Birmingham?' Mrs Turl said. 'What's Birmingham got to do with anything?'

'Haven't you been living in Birmingham?'

'Birmingham?' Mrs Turl said again, as though she were considering a life lived in a foreign country. 'Why, no,' she said, 'I don't think I've ever even been there. Really, did Anna tell you I was in Birmingham?

What can have made her think of Birmingham?'

'I must have misunderstood.'

'No, I don't suppose you did. She wouldn't want you meeting me.' For a moment Tom wondered if she was suggesting Anna might have seen her as a rival for his affections, but he put the thought out of his head. It was ridiculous.

Then she laughed. 'Well, we were never close,' she said, 'But I wonder what else she didn't tell you?'

She took a cigarette from a box on an occasional table and turned to Tom for a light. He didn't have one and looked around for inspiration. She shrugged and lit it herself.

'Well,' she asked, 'what can I do for you?' She smiled again at the expression on Tom's face.

He didn't smile. 'I came to see if you're all right. Are you coping?'

'Of course I'm all right. And I'm coping much better than you look as if you are. Do you always look like this? You look terrible. Have a drink. I'm going to.'

'It's the waiting for news,' Tom said.

'What news?' Mrs Turl was pouring herself a drink.

'I can't sleep. If I close my eyes I see her in some awful situation and I can't reach her to help her.'

'You shouldn't worry,' Mrs Turl said, 'she'll be back in her own good time.'

Tom couldn't believe what he was hearing. 'But you must be out of your mind with worry,' he said.

'Oh, you know what Anna's like, I'm sure she's just gone off somewhere.'

'But something must have happened . . .'

Mrs Turl poured herself another drink.

'I think of her lying trapped in some deserted place,' Tom said, 'or at the bottom of a mineshaft or something . . . waiting for help. And then I lie awake . . . thinking maybe it's because of me. . . .'

'Because of you? How'd she get herself down a mineshaft because of you?' She handed him a whisky.

'Well, I work for a bank. I wonder if she's been kidnapped for a ransom. They might think the bank'd pay.'

Tears came to his eyes. Mrs Turl leaned across and touched his arm. It was the gesture of a woman who had always been good with men when they were in tears. 'You mustn't get so upset,' she said. 'She'll be back. She's just taken off for a while. She was always self-centred like that, never thinking of other people's feelings. Typical of today's younger generation, don't you think?'

Tom noted the way she put him in the same age generation as herself, but he tried not to show that he did.

He said, 'You can't think she's just upped and gone off for a while? She wouldn't do that. She's not a teenager any more.'

'She probably wanted to be by herself for a while.'

Tom got the impression that she was still laughing at him.

'She'd have left a note,' he said. 'Anna wouldn't just disappear.'

'Well, if you say so,' Mrs Turl said, 'but I think it's typical.'

'She'd know I'd be worried.'

'Perhaps that's part of it. She might like the idea of you worrying. Something psychological like that. She was always hogging the lime-light. I don't suppose she's changed, has she? People don't change. They only get older and a bit bored with themselves.'

'Look here,' Tom said, 'I'll tell you what I think. I think she's had some sort of nervous breakdown and she's off somewhere not knowing where she is, or who she is. But I'm not at all satisfied with the way the police are dealing with this. They've no sense of urgency. So I reckon I'm going to have to start inquiries of my own. I'll have to go to France, of course. But maybe she's not in France. If she'd had a nervous break-down and lost her memory, maybe there's some place she'd go, some-where from her past where she was happy?'

'I'm the last person to ask,' Mrs Turl said.

45

'There must be someone, a friend I could start with.'

'You might try Carol Moss,' Mrs Turl said. 'When they were at school Anna was very close to Carol Moss. She spent a lot of time round at Carol's house. Mrs Moss said people thought she was her other daughter. I was busy; I had to go out to work. There was no one else to support us. Carol qualified to be an air hostess, but now she's only a hairdresser. I don't know what these girls have in their minds. They don't seem to have any idea what's best for them.'

'Anna had a good job,' Tom said. 'She was doing very well.'

As Mrs Turl walked beside him to the door, he suddenly thought that he'd spoken of Anna in the past tense, as if she were already lost to him.

7

One of the girls at school used to recite a poem. Anna hadn't thought of it for years but now the lines kept running through her head. *No worst, there is none, pitched past pitch of grief* . . . Carol Moss, that was her name. They used to think it was a joke when she intoned the words in a special solemn voice for comic effect. Such despair was only good for mockery then, they were so young and silly. Anna had never let on, but she'd liked the sound of the words in the poem although it was full of desolation. A priest wrote it, although come to think of it, despair like that must be a sin. Thou shalt not lose hope. It was in all the lessons they gave you, the lessons on life. Carol didn't understood what they meant. Nor did Anna, not then. She could picture Carol, though, still the same big, silly girl with her wide, innocent eyes and her placid expression. She looked like one of those pale-coloured beef cattle from France. Anna used to call her Carol Mouse behind her back and sometimes to her face, too, like the time she said, 'Anna, are you really going to wear that? What will people think of you?' and Anna had said, 'I know what they'll be thinking and it'll be the same thing I'll be thinking'. Carol had been really shocked. She was always being shocked like that.

What had happened between me and Carol Mouse, Anna thought, why did we stop seeing each other?

Carol had gone to be an airline stewardess, but then Anna saw her in the street and she wasn't doing that any more but something Anna forgot. She'd thought it wasn't much to show for all the promise they'd had, but she herself was just as bad. They'd both been stupid. They could have gone to university but they hadn't. The head teacher at school had been angry with them when they told her they didn't want to study any more. They wanted to live Life with a capital letter. The head had smiled in what Anna had thought was a scornful way, but actually it'd probably been pity and not scorn.

Anyway, Carol Mouse's poem kept running through Anna's head because she'd begun to get an inkling of the kind of torment that old priest had been talking about. *More pangs, schooled at forepangs, wilder wring.* She'd thought things couldn't get worse for her than they were, but they had.

It was her dreams. Anna was being tortured by dreams.

It had got to the point where she dreaded going to sleep. She didn't have nightmares: it was worse than that. In the dreams she was happy. She dreamed that she was back in her ordinary life in Godlingford with Tom. She was happy, completely happy. Her nights were spent preparing for their wedding, shopping together at weekends for a bed for their new home, planning colour schemes. It was wonderful creating a setting for the new persona she was taking on as Mrs Pritchard, wife of the assistant bank manager. One night she dreamed they had an argument about whether she should sell her own little house and put the money towards their new place, or let it out so that the rent would cover their mortgage repayments. She was very conscious even in the dream that she had to be careful because she didn't want Tom to ask too many questions about her house. He'd taken it for granted that her father had left it to her when he died. But he didn't, and she didn't want Tom looking at the deeds. Then he'd know that she'd been given the house by someone else, a man she'd once been involved with, a long time ago.

The dream was so vivid she could feel herself sweating, and then

48

she'd told Tom she wanted to start out all new, with no hangovers from her past, even her father, and Tom kissed her and they decided she should sell the house even though the market wasn't booming. She felt so relieved it seemed impossible she could be asleep, and then she and Tom made up and she could *smell* him and she could feel his skin on hers.

And then she woke up in the middle of their lovemaking and none of it was real. In those damned dreams the future was full of promise. Every time she woke she had to face that the future she'd taken for granted had come down to the prospect of endless days chained in a freezing hovel with a monster like Quimper.

There was night after night of this. Blissful happiness, then waking to miserable reality. She could never have explained how horrible it was to be full of joy for a moment until the truth dawned.

There was something else, too, which haunted her mind while she was alone in the daytime. She couldn't get it out of her head that before this had happened to her, she'd not been a very nice person. It wasn't that she could remember actual instances of herself being unkind or lacking in sympathy, because none of her friends, as far as she knew, had ever really suffered. But it was true that when she'd watched the news on television, or read about women raped or harassed, she'd dismissed their suffering as something they'd somehow brought upon themselves. This was hard to face in her present circumstances, and she was ashamed that she'd felt those abused women had somehow made themselves inferior. It wasn't true, and she knew it, but she couldn't feel sorry for them without slightly despising them.

So maybe she deserved what was happening to her. But it didn't make it easier that she found it harder and harder to find anything to like about herself. Now that she knew what it was like to be too terrified to resist, she was consumed with shame for her former self.

In the end, though, all this self-contempt was what gradually gave her the incentive to resist Quimper. Not physically, there was nothing she could do about that, but she thought a lot about Rosa Calvo. Anna was sure Quimper had killed Rosa. Possibly he'd lost his temper and hit her, but more likely, she'd faded away. To fade away and die was the one sure way of escape. What else could she do? What weapons did she have? Anna was doing the same thing herself.

But she wasn't going to let that happen to her. She'd defy the bastard somehow. And she had a weapon. There was Toto.

It was soon clear that Toto was brain-damaged. He was like a young child.

Anna might be able to use him to help herself.

She didn't know how she could do this, but at least it could give her a chance. There was no other way she could see.

She studied Toto. Once Quimper went out in the morning, the boy came down and made himself something to eat. He scowled at Anna, not saying a word.

But he knew things she needed to know.

She tried to make conversation. 'Toto, don't you get bored here? Where do you go for a night out? Where's the nearest town?' He gave her a gormless look as though he didn't understand what she was saying. 'Where does the road go?'

He seemed to be listening, but he still didn't speak. 'How far away are your nearest neighbours? Which way do they live from here?'

He hunched his shoulders and turned away. When she asked again, 'Don't you have any neighbours?' he covered his face with his big hands, but she caught him peeking between his fingers. She did the same and smiled at him. He smiled back.

He looked like a grown young man. He had big hands and feet. He wasn't tall, but he'd got an adult body. In fact, he was almost good-looking, until he smiled and you saw the bad teeth. And when you looked into his eyes, there was nothing there.

Quimper kept the key to the lock on the chain in a drawer in the sideboard on the far side of the kitchen where Anna's thirteen paces did not reach. She had to get Toto to give her that key.

He was pathetic and she felt bad about tricking him. Of course when Quimper found her gone he'd know who'd given her the key. He'd beat the poor dimwit, no doubt about that. Actually Anna thought Quimper was fond of Toto. She'd wondered if he was his father. Anyway she told herself that once she was free she'd bring the police to this house of horrors and Toto would be free of Quimper and that could only be for the good.

Anna had never had anything to do with children. Maybe that was another part of her lack of feeling, her *unnaturalness*! She made the effort with Toto. He didn't respond. She didn't have a knack with kids. Not like Tom. Tom had it. He didn't have to try, children just warmed to him. Children and dogs. They must sense he likes them. Try as Anna might, she didn't like Toto.

She almost gave up hope of winning him over. Then, by chance, she sang a nursery song. He loved it. He wanted to know what it meant. It didn't make any sense in English and it was even more nonsensical translated into French – what, after all, was the French for 'he played knack-knack' and 'paddywack give a dog a bone'? Still, Toto loved it. He wanted her to sing it over and over.

She told him it was a song everyone sang in Godlingford where she came from. She said everyone sang in Godlingford all the time because they were happy. He sat playing with a length of orange twine and taking in that big thought.

She sat staring out the window across the muddy yard. Everything was grey, grey stone walls, grey moor, and a grey mist hanging over the ground, and above it all a grey sky. The kitchen was cold, too. The chill from the flagstone floor struck through the soles of her shoes. The fire in the range had gone out. The metal round her ankle felt like a clamp of ice. She had to remind herself to breathe.

Toto came to her and sat close beside her. She had trouble looking at him. He was dirty and he smelled worse than Quimper.

'Tell me again,' he said, 'about that place.' He meant Godlingford.

Anna started to tell him a story. 'Once upon a time,' she said. Toto stared, his mouth hung open as he listened, revealing the ugly teeth. She took a deep breath and went on, 'I lived in a little house painted a pretty colour like sunlight.'

She told him about Godlingford. She described ordinary life going on there, about Cinderella and her prince, who were her and Tom. She described the town in the rain, bright umbrellas like patchwork on the crowded pavements. Then it was night and the street lights looked orange in the rain and she and Tom were going home to the palace. She was struggling to paint the scenes for him. It was getting harder and harder to make the pictures from that happy life in England superimpose themselves on the enclosing grey walls of stone, with the rain like a fence, and the sky like a grey lid on it. In Godlingford she made the sun shine.

'What did they do then?' Toto asked. He wanted to hear more about Cinderella and the prince.

'They lived happily ever after.'

'In Godlingford?'

'Yes.'

She could tell he was disappointed.

'Why don't you tell me a story?' she said. 'Tell me what you do when you go away?'

Toto looked pleased with himself. He smiled with his horrible teeth. 'I go for money,' he said. 'I go away with the fishermen on the coast to earn wages.'

'What kind of work do you do? Do you work on a boat?'

'I go out on the boat with Joseph into the bay. I check the lobster pots and pull up the nets to see what we've got.'

He spoke about coming home from the coast. 'I like walking over the hills and moors. When it's cold the nights are dark and I rest in the warm straw with the animals.' Like most children, when he wasn't being self-conscious he could describe a thing better than any adult. Anna could see him coming over a hill in the dusk and going into the warm dark of a barn to sleep close to the animals.

But she wasn't going to get sentimental over Toto. 'How long does it take you to get back from the coast?'

He looked vague. 'Many days,' he said. He started to unravel the orange twine he was playing with. 'Look,' he said, 'it's like my hair.' He began to plait the loose threads, then added, 'Sometimes I stay working on the farms, at haymaking and then harvest. I get money.'

'Do you like coming home? Do you like living here with Quimper? Aren't you lonely here?'

He smiled. She kicked herself for asking too much, he wasn't capable of a concept like loneliness.

'I like it better now you've come,' he said.

'Did you like it when Rosa Calvo was here?' she asked. 'Was she pretty to look at?'

Anna had created her own picture of Rosa Calvo. She imagined the kind of woman who would've worn the clothes in the room upstairs. She saw her young, with thick, dark hair, a good-looking, gypsy type. But she wouldn't have looked like that for long. She'd have been worn and haggard, her hands purple with the cold. Anna was getting to look like that. In 1998 Rosa Calvo had been alive. How long did she last after that? Anna's mind raced. She might be only recently dead. She might not be dead. Perhaps she ran off, or she might not even have been Quimper's prisoner. Anna could be getting Rosa Calvo all wrong. Rosa might have been simply a woman who happened to carve her name on a window frame when she was bored, a woman who left because Quimper couldn't satisfy her sexually. Perhaps he'd loved her. But if she ran away, why did she leave her clothes behind?

Anna wasn't looking at Toto when she said Rosa' s name. He jumped up. She thought he was going to hit her. She put up her arms to ward off the blows. He was flailing his arms and stamping. Then he swept everything on the table on to the floor with a crash. He gave a howl like a goaded animal.

She'd blown it. All that effort gone to waste.

She couldn't help it, she started to cry.

He stopped moving and stared at her, curious. 'Why are you crying?' he said.

She said, 'I want to go home.'

'Home to your palace in Godlingford?'

She nodded.

He said, 'I'll give you the key.'

She couldn't believe it. He went to the sideboard and opened the drawer where Quimper kept the key. Then he came and knelt down on the flagstones beside her. He tried to put the key in the padlock on the shackle. His tongue protruded from his mouth as he concentrated. She had to force herself not to grab the key from him. She thought he'd got the wrong key. But he hadn't. The metal bands round her ankle fell away.

At that moment they heard Quimper outside the kitchen door swearing at the dog. There was a yelp of pain and then the sound of Quimper's heavy boots on stone. He came in, shaking off the rain. He caught sight of the dead fire in the grate. 'Imbecile,' he said to Toto. He struck out at him, sending him cowering across the kitchen.

Anna didn't dare move in case he should see that she was free. She prayed he'd turn and go out of the house.

Toto went to the stove and started to riddle the ashes. He was terrified of Quimper's bad mood, almost as frightened as she was.

'Leave that!' Quimper said. 'There's man's work outside. I need your help. Hurry or it'll be dark.' He turned on Anna.

'You,' he said, 'you light the fire.'

Still she didn't dare to move.

'Well?' he said.

'I will,' she said, 'I'll have it ready when you get back.'

He grunted. 'See you do,' he said.

He and Toto went out. She watched them disappear round the corner of the barn, the ugly mongrel following them with its tail tucked between its legs.

At the back door she thought of making a run for the barn and hiding there. But it would not be hard for him to find her there. Instead she stepped out and flattened herself against the wall of the house. Ahead of her, to the right, was the rough track out of the yard leading to the open moorland. To the left the land rose steeply behind the farm into rocky foothills. There would be no road that way. The public road lay down the track across the bog. She had to go that way.

She began to run across the spongy grass.

But she hadn't realized how feeble she was. Her legs were weak. She slipped on the wet ground, stumbled over loose stones. She didn't dare to look back. Gorse spines and the spikes of heather tore at her legs. She was panting and she felt dizzy. Her lungs hurt. She had a stitch in her side. She felt she'd already run a mile, but when she looked back she was less than 200 metres from the house.

And Quimper was there. She saw him come round the side of the barn with the mongrel dog. He was carrying a shotgun. Anna threw herself down behind a clump of gorse, praying he hadn't seen her. She heard him shout at the dog. The animal came loping towards her, its nose to the ground sniffing her trail. She struggled to her feet and tried to run on.

Far ahead, on the dark edge of moorland against grey cloud, she saw the outline of a man. He was tall, in a loose coat, walking slowly away from her. She shouted to him but he didn't turn. 'Help! Help me!' He moved on. She couldn't understand why he didn't hear her. It wasn't as if she were shouting to him in a noisy city street. 'Please,' she yelled, but he was out of earshot.

The dog brought her down. Then Quimper was on her. He dragged her back to the house, cursing. In the kitchen he snapped the metal ring round her ankle. The dog had bitten her and the pain brought tears to her eyes.

Toto was trying to light the fire. 'I didn't do it,' he said, bent over the range 'it wasn't me.' His breath raised a cloud of silvery ash which floated across the room. He handed over the key. Quimper put it in his pocket. 'Halfwit,' he said, and punched Toto on the side of the head. Then he punched him again, this time in the face. Toto's nose started to bleed.

Anna wished he'd turn on Quimper. He was much younger, and very strong. If he attacked him and held him down, she could loop her chain round Quimper's neck and strangle him. But Toto simply stood there until Quimper stopped hitting him, giving him a final cuffing in the same casual manner as when he cuffed the dog.

She blamed Toto, but she was angry with herself. She'd wasted her best chance to escape. She'd been stupid. She hadn't realized how weak she was. She'd sat around feeling sorry for herself instead of forcing herself to exercise to prepare to take any chance she got to escape.

She must look at everything that happened to her for an opportunity she could use. She must try to eat the food Quimper gave her; she must exercise as best she could to build up some strength. *No hope, there is none,* that old priest, Gerard Manley Hopkins, wrote in his poem, but she wouldn't believe it. It was up to her to find it.

She knew Quimper would make her pay for what she'd done when he came to her in the night, but though he could force her to do the disgusting things he wanted, she felt that he had lost some of his power over her. She'd had a chance. There would be another.

And she had a real reason for hope. The tall man might have heard her cry out to him. He might have thought at the time he'd heard a hawk or a fox, but afterwards he'd wonder . . . He might've looked back when Quimper was dragging her away. If he'd seen something, if he thought perhaps he'd seen a man with a woman. . . . It might come to him later. He might know that an Englishwoman was missing. He might begin to think. Oh, let him at least mention to someone that he heard something unusual.

8

Tom was late into the office. Not more than a few minutes late, but already Mr Tetley, the manager, was asking for him. Nigel Duffy, the other assistant manager, had met him at the lift to tell him with some relish of Mr Tetley's impatience.

Then he saw the expression on Tom's face. 'Are you OK?' he asked. 'You look awful.'

'Migraine,' Tom said. It was the only thing he could think of.

'Can I do anything?' Duffy was suddenly all kindness. He was an ambitious man, and he had a fixed belief that the Masons would block his promotion in the bank. He worried that Tom might be a Mason. But he warmed even to Tom when he looked as though he might need comfort or advice.

Tom wanted only to be rid of him. He felt sick and cold with shock. He knew why Mr Tetley wanted to see him.

He went into his office and shut the door before Duffy could follow him. He would go to see Mr Tetley in a moment, but he had to think.

He opened his attache case and took out his regular *Daily Telegraph*. Underneath it the garish masthead of the awful tabloid glared up at him. He closed the lid of the case to hide it.

As a rule, Tom never bought those disgusting tabloids. He wouldn't have known about the story if the newsagent on the corner hadn't been a fellow member of the tennis club and warned him about it.

Mr Tetley would have to wait. Tom sat at his desk and put his head in his hands, trying to shut out the huge black headline which seemed to be imprinted on his vision. Mrs Turl, 'Mother of Missing Good Time Gal', had held nothing back. Tom asked himself what kind of imagination could make up things like that? The newspaper must have conned the woman. 'Teenage Tart Bonked Pop Band In Drugs Orgy'. Anna's mother, her own mother, had painted a picture of her daughter, of his Anna, as practically a whore.

Tom shuddered at the thought of the word. That wasn't even the worst of it. According to Mrs Turl, Anna had been a teenage terror who mugged old ladies and shoplifted to feed her drug habit. She slept around with criminals and any weirdo she could pick up around the wilder extremes of the music business. At 20 she had taken up with a rap artist and lived in squalor with him for a year until he was killed in a brawl in a Brixton bar.

The newspaper had illustrated its story with pictures. One showed a young girl, topless, leaning forward with her lips pursed ready for a kiss, her thumbs stuck into the elastic top of very skimpy shorts like a cowboy holstering his guns. In another head only shot, the same girl appeared with her tongue out to show off a metal stud. She wore what seemed to Tom to be ear-rings dangling from a nose ring. The girl did not look to him in the least like Anna. If Mrs Turl had been trying to jog someone's memory about seeing Anna since she disappeared, Tom thought she had not helped at all. All the same, he had to admit, if those photographs were really of a younger Anna, he found himself daunted at how much he did not know about her.

The newspaper made much of the torments Mrs Turl had suffered as the mother of such a daughter. She was still suffering. Police in England and France had not closed the case, but they had called off an international search for the missing girl which had already cost taxpayers several hundred thousand pounds. The expense of searching for such a girl, that was the nub of the story.

The telephone on Tom's desk rang. It was Mr Tetley, and from the tone of his voice left Tom in no doubt that he had seen the story. Tom could not put it off any longer.

He went into the manager's office. 'It's all lies,' he said. 'They must've made Anna's mother believe any publicity would help.'

'I don't see that even a distraught mother could think that publicity of such a nature could help,' Mr Tetley said.

Tom tried to tell himself that Mr Tetley was being over-judgemental but he couldn't. He agreed with him. 'It's lies,' he said. 'She'll sue.'

'But they've got pictures,' Mr Tetley said.

'Well, the pictures don't prove anything really, do they?' Tom said. He was beginning to feel angry. Mostly he was angry at the newspaper people, and then at Mrs Turl, but Mr Tetley was in front of him putting into words the things he didn't want to admit he was thinking himself and Tom couldn't forgive him for that. 'They're just pictures of a teenage girl having a good time with her friends.'

'My teenage daughters don't look like that when they're photographed,' Mr Tetley said. 'Nor do their friends.'

Tom did not know what to say. He no longer heard what Mr Tetley was saying. He couldn't take in what was happening. It was as though they were talking about someone he'd never met. People he'd never met and didn't know were saying these things about his Anna, and all he could do was say they were lying. But why? Why would Anna's mother say things like that about her own daughter, even for money? Why would anyone want to say such things about a sweet girl like Anna?

Tom left Mr Tetley, who was a small middle-aged man with a bristling little moustache, and went back to his office feeling as though he'd done ten rounds with a heavyweight boxer.

He tried to think what he should do next. He couldn't even get up the courage to go to the machine for a cup of coffee. His colleagues would know about the newspaper story. All the juniors would have read it. He couldn't face their little sniggers, not yet. And then there was his mother. She wouldn't see the paper, but someone would be sure to tell her. He dreaded the confrontation he must have with her.

Tom wondered if he'd made a mistake staying on at home living with his mother. He knew it made an old man out of him, a joke figure. But she'd be lonely if he left. She talked about her friends behaving oddly once their children left home. It would be different when he left to get married, she'd have him and Anna close by, and grandchildren coming soon. The arrival of grandchildren would surely make her like Anna better; perhaps she might even start loving her. Or so he had always hoped. There wasn't much chance of that now. He was sure that the newspaper had got their story wrong. They'd twisted what Mrs Turl said, no doubt about that. Or perhaps she'd even gone along with them and made up what she thought they wanted to hear. She would think she was helping Anna, keeping her disappearance in the headlines. He decided that that was the case, even if it was unlikely.

His own mother, though, would believe every word they printed to make Anna look like some latter-day houri. One of his mother's friends would make sure she got to see the story. And his mother, Tom knew, believed every word she read in the newspapers, because it was in print. That was the way she'd been brought up.

He thought, I'll have to sue. That's the only way to prove it's all lies they've printed. But suppose he couldn't prove his case, he'd make everything much worse Not, of course, that he thought they weren't lies; the problem was proving it when he knew so little about Anna's past.

Tom picked up the telephone and dialled the number Mrs Turl had given him for the hairdresser's where Carol Moss worked. Carol Moss had trouble understanding who he was. He had trouble, in the state he was in, explaining the reason for his call.

She was mildly surprised to hear from Anna's fiancé, but she agreed to meet him.

'Where?' he said.

'Oh, I don't know,' she said. 'I can't see you here. I presume you'd prefer somewhere private. How about my flat? After work.'

When he was silent, she said, 'Don't be afraid.'

'Afraid?'

'I've got two flatmates, you'll be safe.'

'Oh,' he said. He couldn't think in this jokey way.

The moment he put the phone down, he wished he had never made the call. He didn't want to meet Carol Moss. He had hoped that she might reinforce his belief that Anna would not have run away without a word, whatever the police might think. And if something had upset her and she had taken herself off to think things over, he thought Carol might have an idea where she'd go. But that disgusting newspaper story had changed things. He couldn't ask the girl if those terrible things were true. If they weren't, she'd think he was betraying Anna by doubting her. If they were, she probably wouldn't tell him. He would look more of a fool than he did already.

At one point in the day he had tried ringing her again to cancel their appointment. Carol wasn't there, though, and he hadn't wanted to leave a message in case it looked as though they had a date. Tom put inverted commas round the word date, even in his head. Simply meeting Carol couldn't do any more harm than had been done already. If the worst came to the worst and Carol was a ghastly little tart who confirmed everything the newspaper said, well, he would have to deal with that as best he could.

So, in the early evening, Tom drove across Godlingford to Southwood to meet Carol. She'd said she would be home by seven-thirty. He passed endless rows of neat little houses, then the ugly blocks of 1960s' flats built up along the London Road. He thought how bleak and mean life looked, compared with the area where he lived, where Godlingford was still a pretty Surrey village beyond the grasp of the commuter belt.

63

Carol lived on a long stretch of ribbon development where Godlingford turned into the Outer London suburb of Southwood. The houses were all the same, three-bedroomed semi-detached villas with wrap-around front windows and a hard standing at the front for a car. They had been built in the 1930s and since then they had stared blankly at each other across the dual carriageway. The monotony was punctuated only by intermittent mock-Victorian red-brick public houses at road junctions, all of which, or so it seemed to Tom, were called The Halfway House.

As he crawled along the kerb looking for Carol's house, he was irritated by the pretentiousness which made people living in such places drop numbers for pathetic names like Bellavista or Blenheim, as if such nonsense was going to change the fact of their cramped homes. But, he thought, maybe it was a way they told which house was theirs. The names were probably easier to recall than numbers. Tom couldn't understand how this could be, but he was well aware how hard people found even remembering a simple PIN number. Still, the wretched names were no help to him.

When he found that he had overrun the number of Carol's house, he had to drive back towards Godlingford to find a roundabout so he could get back to the right side of the carriageway. What a way to live, he thought. He'd always thought of life being comfortable and pleasant in the quiet suburbs of Surrey, but obviously it wasn't always so. Perhaps if he saw the ugly houses in bright sunlight he would feel differently.

Carol Moss lived in the top half of a house divided into flats. He rang the upper bell on the door too long and too loud because he was now in such a bad mood. He hated the wretched house. He hated Mrs Turl because without her he wouldn't be here. He hated Carol because he'd asked her to see him and now he didn't want to meet her at all. He was tempted to turn and run before she opened the door. She can't help it, he thought. She didn't build the house. She just had to live in it. That didn't necessarily make her mean-spirited.

When the door opened, not very wide, he saw a bright blonde's face. She wasn't wearing any make-up and she had a friendly smile. She didn't look like anyone's idea of a teenage terror, or a drug fiend. 'Sorry,' she said, 'I was washing my hair. You're early.' She unhooked the chain and opened the door wide. Her blonde hair was quite short and curly; probably, he thought, because it was still wet.

She looked as nervous as he felt. She was standing on the step above him and she held her head down as if she was shy, looking up at him. She was what his mother would describe as a big girl, but she had large eyes that made her attractive. He could imagine her as Anna's friend. He had a sentimental picture of them being schoolgirls together. He wished he could have known them then. But, of course, when he was at an age when he would have noticed girls in the park, they'd have been at nursery school. Once again he felt old; he was nearly middle-aged. Carol seemed terribly young. She was the same age as Anna, but he had grown used to Anna and started to think of her as a contemporary of his; at least, he had until now; since she'd gone missing he'd been horribly aware that she was a young woman of a different generation from himself.

'You found it first time?' Carol asked.

'The second time,' he said.

She was making small talk as she led him upstairs. She was tall and slim and once again he found himself following the backside of a desirable but untouchable woman. Mrs Turl had been alarmingly sexy, but after the initial shock of Anna's mother being so young, he had tried not to look at her. He felt guilty, too, looking at Carol. He raised his eyes to study something less disturbing than the generous curves of her backside. He looked at the small of her back, her shoulders and the nape of her neck, which was covered in downy tendrils of hair. He stumbled. What a fool I am, he thought, an utter fool. He frowned, but he wasn't thinking of himself stumbling on the stair behind this blonde who was Anna's girlhood friend, he was thinking of what the newspaper had said about Anna. Tom felt he had been robbed of something. He had felt it ever since reading the paper. He had been brooding about it since then. It was something very old-fashioned and masculine: he felt he had been robbed of his honour. He should've gone to Canary Wharf and confronted the newspaper editor and picked him up and thrown him across the room and to hell with what the police might say.

The upper floor of the house was cramped but he could see that it was homely. The main bedroom of the original house had been converted into a sitting-room and kitchen. Carol explained that she had a room of her own and that the two other girls shared the larger of the bedrooms.

'I'm squeezed into the small one,' Carol said, 'but it's better than sharing. You've got to have your own space sometimes.' Tom felt cramped standing; he scarcely seemed to have enough room to move. Of course he was a big bloke, but he wondered how people put up with never having enough room to move freely.

The flatmates weren't home from work. Tom looked out from the uncurtained window while Carol made coffee, and for the first time since Anna went missing he felt comfortable, despite the smallness of the room, or perhaps because of it. He felt cosy, and if that was silly, still he felt it. He looked at the faceless houses across the way. There was a double line of traffic crawling both ways on the dual carriageway, it looked to him like seeing his side of the road reflected in a mirror. He would never have imagined feeling glad to be in a room like this; then he realized why, it was new to him, a place with no association with Anna – at least, until they started talking about her, it would have no association with Anna.

'How do you get across to the other side?' he asked Carol when she brought him a mug of coffee.

'You don't, really,' she said, sitting down in front of the gas fire with her legs tucked under her. Her big strong legs were more muscular than Mrs Turl's, healthier, younger. He tried to pretend he hadn't been looking at Carol and thinking what a fine, upstanding specimen she was.

'There's a subway to get to the other side,' she said. 'I use it in the morning, to catch the bus to work, but I wouldn't go through there after dark. Gangs of teenagers hang out there, and at night it's full of drunks and druggies.'

Tom shook his head. He'd never realized that even for a girl like Carol, who looked as though she could take care of herself all right, even going out at night was an act of deliberate courage. He wondered about his mother. She scarcely ever went out of the house on her own. It had never occurred to him that she might even want to. And what about Mrs Turl? Tom thought Mrs Turl probably caused more menace than she suffered.

Carol said, 'You wanted to talk about Anna?' She still kept her head down, looking up with only her eyes. He supposed it was a mannerism of a tall girl who was basically shy. 'I don't know if I'll be any help. It's some time since I last saw her. To talk to, anyway. I've seen the Golden Tours posters, of course.'

'Have you seen the story in the newspaper?' He hated asking the question; it seemed to give credence to the tabloid's preposterous lies about Anna. He mumbled and then had to repeat the question because she didn't understand what he was saying.

'You shouldn't believe everything you read in the newspapers,' she said.

He was astonished that she could take the story so lightly. He took a deep breath. 'It's lies,' he said. 'Isn't it?'

Carol gave him a direct look for the first time. 'It doesn't matter if it is or it isn't,' she said, 'the effect's the same: people always believe the worst. Anyway, they'll forget about it by tomorrow.'

'But what about the effect on Anna's life? They called her a . . .' He couldn't say the word. 'They made her out to be promiscuous,' he said.

'They've ruined her reputation.' Even he could hear that he sounded stuffy and out of touch.

Carol didn't answer the question. 'There's nothing you can do, Tom. It's the twist they put on things. You read those stories and there's nothing there that couldn't be said about most lively teenagers. Anna wasn't a virgin. You must've known that. She did live with some sort of a pop singer for a few months and she probably smoked the odd joint at a party. Who hasn't?'

'I haven't,' Tom said.

Carol smiled. She took his empty mug and hers to the sideboard and busied herself opening a bottle of wine. She came back with two full glasses and sat down beside him on the sofa.

'Here,' she said, handing him one. 'And actually nor have I.'

'Thanks,' he said, taking the glass. Then he asked, 'What are people going to think?'

'About you and me having a glass of wine together?'

Tom didn't laugh. 'About Anna.' Carol could laugh it off, but the problem was a serious one. He knew what people did think, people like Mr Tetley, and he knew that it mattered very much. Mr Tetley had said, ' It's not at all the right impression for the bank . . . prejudice your promotion . . . What will people think. . . ?'

Carol took a swig of the wine. 'Look,' she said, 'I think it's you has the problem, not Anna. Even if every word of that story is true, which it isn't, it isn't saying Anna did anything so dreadful. It was all ages before she even met you, you know. She's still exactly the same person she's always been; she hasn't turned into some kind of monster overnight.' She paused and then demanded, 'Has she?'

Tom couldn't meet her eyes. He couldn't answer the question. He was embarrassed because deep down he wasn't sure that she hadn't touched on the real thing he couldn't face. He loved Anna and so, because he loved her, he had seen her as the person he wanted to make into his wife, the wife of a future bank manager. Had wishful thinking made him delude himself? He'd seen and known only what suited him. Why had he never pressed her about her mother, and other things, like sex and why she was such a marvellous lover? Why should he? He didn't want to know more than the fact of their happiness together. But he had a niggling suspicion that other men would've wanted to know. Perhaps he'd had some instinct not to rock the boat. She'd gone along with it. She'd seemed to want to be the right wife for him. But she was young. Perhaps she hadn't realized.

He heard Carol's voice and realized he had not been listening to her.

'I don't believe Anna ran away like the police think,' she said. 'The Anna I knew would tell you straight out. Something's happened to her.'

'Yes,' Tom said. 'That's why I came, really, except that damned newspaper story distracted me. I'm going to France to look for her.' Then he said, 'Will you come with me?'

He hadn't been thinking about it and it just came out. 'I don't speak French,' he said. 'You do, don't you?'

'Yes,' she said, 'but when are you going?'

She couldn't drop everything, take time off work. But it was true she thought something bad had happened to Anna: she wasn't saying that simply to comfort Tom.

'As soon as possible,' Tom said.

'OK,' she said, and surprised herself as she said it.

69

9

Toto was disappointed. The bitch was too thin. She didn't look like Joseph's woman. When he was working on the fishing boat Toto shared Joseph's house. One night, Toto thought Joseph's woman was dying. He watched Joseph with the woman. It burst hot out of Toto and then was cold on his stomach. He watched them every night after that, scarcely trying to smother his own orgasmic noises.

Now he watched this other bitch. There was a hole in the wall. He watched Quimper at night with her. Sometimes he saw nothing because Quimper sat on the bed with his back to him and he couldn't see her.

He liked to watch her but she was getting too thin. He found he had to think of other times with Joseph's well-covered whore to come off. He looked on as this scrawny bitch ran her fingers through her hair. He could see the loose dark threads come away in her fingers. Her eyes went big, then there were tears. But she was making no sound. She bent forward, clinging to the rim of the basin. She went on her knees, leaning her forehead against the enamel edge of the bowl. When she pulled herself to her feet. She looked ugly, with swollen eyes. He saw her mouth open.

His penis was still soft. He closed his eyes and thought of one night when what he saw so turned him on he'd come where he stood and his come had hit the wall and left a long dribbling stain on the wallpaper.

Toto had heard the springs of the bed creak. He'd got his eye to the hole in the wall to see Quimper holding something metal. Toto could smell petrol. Quimper had a petrol funnel in his right hand and he was holding the bitch down with his body while he held the lips of her cunt open and worked the funnel into her body.

The bitch was screaming. He could see her face, the mouth open and her eyes squeezed shut. She lashed out at Quimper but he knocked her back down. He, too, was watching her face to see the pain and panic she was feeling. When he drew the funnel out, she gasped. She rolled on her side, doubled up with pain. He pushed her over on her face and then shoved it between her buttocks. Then Toto could hold it no longer and his eyes closed as the come spurted. When he looked again, Quimper had gone and the bitch lay like something broken on the bloodstained sheet.

10

Tom and Carol had taken the route from the ferry which Tom had worked out from the map Anna would have taken to the Château de Goriac. Tom stopped in every village, accosted everyone they passed on the road. He was obsessed. Like a latter-day Ancient Mariner he forced anyone and everyone to listen to his story about Anna disappearing. He showed Anna's photograph, describing her to baffled French people.

Carol translated for him. It seemed to her, listening to his description of Anna, that he had never really looked at her. He had such an old-fashioned notion of her. Carol thought that if anyone had seen Anna, they wouldn't recognize her as the person he described. She tried to be more realistic as she translated for him. She told them Anna was dark and sexy-looking and the Frenchmen smiled, nodding their heads, while the women looked at Tom in a certain way, and then at her, as though they were surprised that he could have a girl like the one Carol was describing when Carol herself was plainly so much more suitable.

And I am, Carol told herself, and this is hell. I wish I'd never come. But then I wouldn't've met him. I wish I could go home. But then I'd never see him again. I wish . . . I wish . . . Carol stopped short of wishing Anna dead. Oh, God, she thought, I'm sorry, Anna, I can't help it, it's nothing personal. I didn't want it to happen, but I love him, I love him, I love him.

Each time she translated another outpouring of his love for Anna, each time she saw the look on his face as he showed her photograph, Carol felt sick. She could never inspire the kind of love he had for Anna.

Beyond the car window the Breton landscape was ugly and depressing. She'd decided that the moment they drove away from the ferry port. She hadn't really looked at the scenery since. She stared out of the window to keep herself from looking at Tom. She wanted to look at him. She wanted to stare at him until she'd had her fill of him, of the way his hair grew, of how the skin round his eyes creased when he was tired, how he smiled when he turned to her and said 'Once more into the breach, dear friend' whenever he stopped the car to start another search for witnesses.

They had spent three nights in Brittany already. Carol did not know what she could do. She could not offer herself to him. If he'd been different, he might have made love to her because she brought him closer to Anna, but Tom wasn't like that. If he came to her at night, it would be to talk about Anna. She hoped for that, at least. But ever since arriving in Brittany she'd waited alone in bed at night for a tap on the door, wishing she had the courage to go and tap on his. He was, after all, probably lying awake staring into the dark and feeling lonely. It was ridiculous. She was ridiculous. But she had known from the first time they met that she and Tom were made for each other. They should've met and fallen in love and lived happily ever after like millions of people like themselves. Instead, they'd got involved in a children's fairytale: he was bewitched by a phantom, a woman who did not really exist. But he would never believe that.

Carol told herself, Anna never was the right woman for him, but Tom believes she is. And if Anna were dead, Carol thought, it wouldn't bring him any closer to loving me.

She dared to look at his profile. He was concentrated on the road. It was raining, blowing a gale. Don't worry, Anna, Carol told Anna in her head, you're the only one he's thinking about, I know that.

He looked so sad she had to look away.

'According to the police,' Tom said, 'it was a night just like this that Anna disappeared.'

Carol said nothing. They were driving west, retracing the phantom Anna's journey, the phantom Anna's no doubt fictional journey. But he had to do something, after all, he couldn't simply sit in Surrey. But it was getting ridiculous, such a waste of time.

And the weather was turning worse. Sleet, hurled by a furious gale, snapped at the windscreen.

'How far to the hotel?' Carol asked. Her voice wasn't quite steady. She was tired. She was also frightened. She couldn't see anything ahead beyond a bank of spray. Tom slowed the car. A large vehicle was passing them. She saw the huge metal nuts of a lorry's wheel through the smeared car window. It threw up spray. She gave a little gasp and braced herself.

Tom, without taking his eyes from the road, leant towards her and gave her knee a squeeze. She touched his knuckles with her fingertips. A natural enough gesture between two people, she thought, but she didn't trust herself to speak. It's only proximity, she told herself, but even so . . . And they would be blamed for it. No one would believe they weren't lovers. Of course they'd think that, back in Godlingford, seeing a man and woman going off to France together. They'd probably laugh at her and think he'd grabbed the first girl he could get on the rebound because Anna had run off on him. Carol understood that. She knew that Tom was too innocent to realize. She couldn't tell him. Just as she couldn't tell him he was too innocent when it came to Anna. He believed all the lies she'd told him. Carol knew that the lies showed how much Anna cared for him. Men were too thick to see that, but it went without saying among women. Anna wouldn't have taken the trouble to tell him so many lies if she didn't love him. But now he'd got this detective thing into his head and he was finding out things he'd rather not

75

know. Carol agonized about it. She wanted him to be put off Anna, but at the same time she felt a rat for not defending her friend.

'Anna must've been terrified, driving in this,' she said, 'I'd be scared stiff.'

'Anna didn't like motorways,' he said. 'Her car was always packing up in the rain, the spray got into the electrics. She was always having to get off the M25 and take quieter roads.'

'Well the electrics obviously didn't pack up that night,' Carol said. 'They'd have found her car.' And again she thought, this is a waste of time, I shouldn't have come. Anna isn't here, if she's in France she's somewhere South in the sun, that's her style. She got bored with the idea of being a bank manager's wife and took off in a way that would finish it in a highly melodramatic way. 'Oh, I wish, I wish,' she whispered under her breath.

'If I'd been Anna,' she said aloud, 'I'd have come off this awful road at the first turning.'

'You're right,' Tom said, 'that's just what she'd have done, got off this before the engine conked out.'

'Take the next turn then,' Carol said. 'Why not?'

On a small road, she thought, I might feel as though I'm really in France. On a motorway in the rain I could be anywhere. She wanted to be somewhere with a big bottle of wine on the table and a man in a striped jersey playing the accordion. She wanted to pretend that Anna didn't exist, that she never had existed. She wanted to be Anna, beloved of Tom.

Tom took the next slip road. He drove as though the car was a rugby ball he was kicking into touch. 'At least I can see where I'm going,' he said.

Not that there was much to look at. The daylight had gone, everything was dim, only the black outline of some low, sawn-off hills showed against the grey sky. The road crossed yet another stretch of dingy moorland covered in a dark scrawl of sodden heather.

They drove in silence. A village appeared, at least a small gathering of houses on either side of the road. They seemed uninhabited, boards were nailed over the windows. It was all so desolate Carol felt like screaming. Why was everything in the world so ugly?

'It's not my idea of France,' she said. Her idea of France was the heat of Provence, with old men playing boules under the chestnut trees, while she sat at a table outside a café, getting sloshed and feeling romantic.

Tom had suddenly become cautious at the wheel, he was moving at a crawl, as though it was his first time driving on the right. Maybe it was, she thought. He was Surrey man. He wouldn't be romantic in the shade of a chestnut tree on a hot day in Provence. He'd get sunburned and his nose would peel and his legs would be white in shorts. He'd probably wear socks with sandals, Carol thought. She smiled as though that was the way things really were. But it isn't, she told herself, and fought to stop her eyes flooding with tears.

Through the rain they saw a bare light bulb swinging on a cable slung like a washing-line between two buildings. This cast a shadowy glow across a small forecourt with petrol pumps.

They pulled in and Carol got out even in all that wind and rain to stretch her legs. Tom sounded his horn and slammed the car door as he got out, but there was no response from the darkened building. He called out and pounded on the garage doors, a crazed metallic drumming. Carol thought, I'm mad to be here with him. Even if Anna's really ditched him, he'll never get over her. And as for me, will I get over him?

Carol wished she was at home telling someone the story of this nightmare trip; she'd make it sound funny. No, she told herself, it's not funny. I couldn't tell anyone about this.

A beam of light appeared around the side of the building. A young girl stepped into the shifting circle of light from the swinging bulb. She spoke to Tom, who looked blank and turned to Carol.

'She says they're closed,' Carol said. Then she said to the girl, in French, 'We want to ask a few questions.'

'We're closed,' the girl said again.

'We're looking for the Château de Goriac,' Tom said in English. He held out the photograph of Anna. It got wet in the rain. The girl paid little attention to the photo.

'Thirty kilometres or so down the road,' she said to Carol while Tom kept asking her in English if she'd seen the woman in the photo. The girl didn't understand him. She thought he was still talking about the way to Goriac. 'Englishmen are all the same,' she said in French to Carol, 'they always expect places to be nearer than they are.'

'Do you remember this woman?' Carol asked. She gestured Tom to hold up the photograph for the girl to see. 'Have you ever seen her?'

The girl took it and held it up to the light.

'No,' the girl said. She handed the photo back to Tom.

'Some time ago now,' Carol said. 'A woman in a red Panda car?'

Tom said, 'Tell her she's beautiful. Tell her she's tall and slim. She couldn't forget seeing her.'

'I wouldn't really call her slim, and she's quite small. About here,' Carol said to him, holding her hand up to show how much shorter Anna was than herself.

'No,' Tom said, 'she's taller than that. I'm sure she is.'

Carol said in French to the girl, 'She's a woman my age.'

'English?' the girl asked, and Carol started. The way the girl said 'English', she recognized Anna in the photo, Carol was sure of it. I saw her face, she recognized Anna, she told herself.

'There's been no one English like that one,' the girl said. 'Not while I've been here.' In spite of the shadows Carol thought that the girl's expression turned sly. Then the girl said, 'She looks familiar. Is she famous?'

'No,' Carol said, 'she's not anyone. She's this man's fiancée.'

'What are you saying?' Tom asked.

'She asked if Anna is famous.'

'She might have seen her picture in the paper,' Tom said. Carol translated this.

The girl said, 'In the paper? How come so if she's not famous?'

'I told you, she's not famous,' Carol repeated. 'She's missing.'

'She's the one the police were here about, then?' the girl said. 'They interrogated my sister, Sylvie, the other day. But she'd not seen her.'

'Do you and your sister serve here?' Carol asked.

'We all do,' the girl said.

'How many sisters do you have?' Carol asked.

'Five of us, and Jeanne, but she's just a baby. But I wasn't here when the police came to question Sylvie.' She stared at Tom, plainly curious. 'Our Sylvie went missing once,' the girl said. 'We thought the worst, of course. But she'd only met a man from Brest and run off to be with him. He dumped her and she came back.'

'What is she talking about?' Tom said.

'About her sister who ran away with a man from Brest. Didn't she leave a note?' Carol asked the girl.

'What are you saying?' Tom asked. Carol told him. 'For God's sake,' he said, 'what are we listening to this for?'

The girl said, 'She didn't leave a note because we were what she was running away from.' Then she added, 'I can ask my sisters about this woman if you want.'

Carol repeated this in English. Tom sighed. He asked, 'How many sisters does she have?'

'Six.'

'Six? Good God! We'll be here all night asking them.'

Carol looked at him. Was this a sign that he was bored at last with his quest? He was tired out after the journey. She'd offered to share the driving and he'd said the car was only insured for him, but she knew he'd said that because he wouldn't have liked being driven by a woman.

'Oh,' he said, 'what's the point? Six daughters living in there.' He

79

looked at the dark house in the rain. 'She'd know. They'd have talked about it, wouldn't they? It would be an exciting thing, an Englishwoman stopping at the station and then going missing.'

Poor Tom, he sounded exhausted, but he was making sense at last. Still, the girl had recognized Anna, but probably only from a newspaper photo. 'Come on,' she said, taking his arm. 'We can always come back.'

11

Anna thought, I hadn't realized how much people take hope for granted. Oh, I know there have never been so many victims of depression, but even then a lot of them can take a pill and expect to feel better in a little while. Which is a form of hope, isn't it?

It hadn't taken long after her attempt to run away before she began to realize that hope was something she had to work at. She wanted to keep it, she positively needed it if she was going to survive; but it was like trying to carry water in cupped hands. Any little hope she had kept seeping away.

The thought of the man she'd seen in the distance kept her going through the unspeakable night. Quimper had from the start abused her physically in ways she couldn't believe. Looking at the man, a total peasant, she found it impossible to imagine how he could conceive the things he did to her. She couldn't help wondering what kind of state he must be in, working round the farm seeing sexual connotations for the most ordinary and everyday things. She told herself she'd read about perversion; she'd indulged, too, when she was with a particular man in her past, in a little mild experimentation. But Quimper was different, a real monster. He was violent and he liked to torture. She could feel him respond with pleasure when she cried out in pain. He's a sadist, she thought.

Her worst doubts that she would ever escape crept in with the cold light of early morning. Before Quimper came to take her down to the kitchen, she stared at herself reflected in the freckled glass of Rosa Calvo's mirror. She called it Rosa Calvo's mirror because she found faint comfort in the thought that another living human face had appeared there.

In the past, she'd been rather proud of her body. Tom always told her she was beautiful, and he didn't just mean her face. That was quite a compliment from him, because even mentioning anything physical about a woman made him embarrassed. He'd discuss minute details of the state of his muscular structure with other rugby players, but the vaguest mention of the female form made him positively coy.

She thought, he wouldn't be embarrassed by the womanliness of my body now. Well, he would, he'd be mortified by how ugly it was. It didn't look like the female form, let alone the female form divine.

She was very thin and flat, the hipbones hideously prominent, breasts drooping. Her face was gaunt, covered in sores. She was sure these were caused by being rubbed against various filthy parts of Quimper's hairy body.

Suddenly she was clawing at her skin. The body in the mirror repelled her; she felt compelled to deface it.

Her nails were too soft, they left only faint red tracks, they did not tear the skin. 'Did you look like this?' she asked Rosa Calvo. 'How long before you faded right away?'

No one would come to save her now. She wasn't worth saving. There was no use left for anyone in the thing she'd become. Would Alain Dulac care to find her now? She'd held the romantic name of the guide and fisherman mentioned in Quimper's newspaper in her mind, she'd had visions of him, young and strong, rescuing her. Forget it, she told herself, no one is out there trying to find me.

Bastards, she thought, they're not even trying. They've given up and forgotten about me. If that was all it mattered to anyone, I'll use the broken mirror to cut my wrists. I could escape that way. But then she thought, that isn't right. To hell with them, I do matter. I matter to myself. That's what counts in self-help books.

And she thought, yes, my mind works in clichés. She told herself, while there's life, there's hope. Hope's the one weapon I've got that Quimper can't kill for me. I'll have to do that for myself, and that I'm not going to do.

With that new resolution, she was suddenly aware of her surroundings, and herself inside them. The grey flagstones on the floor struck damp through her feet. She heard water dripping from the walls of the well. When she put her hand against the rough walls, the bare stone felt clammy.

But outside the kitchen window she saw spring sun. She began to weep, but they weren't bitter tears of despair or self-pity. She wept because she couldn't run out and breathe fresh air or feel the warm wind on her face; the tears were the only way she could express the life force returning to revive her spirit. The sun made it seem the whole world had woken up, and now she, too, had emerged from a long hibernation.

The granite buildings round the yard had an iridescent sheen in the sun. Boris, the black and white mongrel, lay flat on his side against the door of a shed, the dark part of his unkempt coat gleaming blue in the sudden strong light. She sat and stared through the dirty glass. Little birds flashed across the sky. Then one great black crow, a bird of ill omen, strutted across the yard looking very full of itself. Another large bird, a hawk, was winding its way slowly up a thermal. And then another and another. Four, five, six hawks riding the wind. Anna's throat ached. It was painful, seeing this, being forced apart from it. She began to burn with resentment against Quimper. He had taken control of her life and he had no right. She thought of how everything she'd ever valued was slowly drifting away from her. Tom would be starting each new day thinking a little less about her. She was drifting, slowly drifting out of his thoughts, out of everyone's thoughts. She'd let it happen, in a way, because she didn't know how to stop it. But from that moment, she withdrew compliance. Anna Turl was no one's patsy, and she would prove it, even if only to herself. There must be a way, and the thing to do was to find it. She said aloud, 'I'll find it.'

12

Tom waited for Carol in the bar of the Château de Goriac. All that driving and the weather had got him down, but he felt more cheerful now that he had washed and changed out of wet clothes. He was almost enjoying himself. Except, the last time I came here, he thought, Anna and I were going to spend the weekend together. He had a moment of sexual longing for Anna, like a small electrical charge, a flicker. He imagined her as if she'd actually been here that weekend and had come running down the hotel steps to greet him. Then they would have gone upstairs. He had wanted her so much after a week apart. That weekend they'd been great lovers in his head, sitting at the bar.

He ordered a whisky. 'Last time I was here—' Tom said to the barman who spoke English, but the barman was busy with another customer.

Someone came up behind him at the bar and Tom turned and saw a tall man with white hair and deepset pale-blue eyes. Tom thought he looked like a Scotsman, a Highland chieftain, or maybe a ghillie, but when he spoke English his accent was all French.

'You remember? I'm Alain Dulac,' the tall man said. 'We had a drink, in the little bar in the square in Goriac.'

Tom remembered him then, the trout fisherman. The Frenchman had been drunk and Tom had got drunk with him, it was embarrassing not being able to recall what he'd said or done in this old man's company. Tom was always embarrassed when he met people who had seen him drunk. He wasn't teetotal but he tried not to overdo it, he didn't like feeling he'd lost control. He liked to be responsible.

'Yes,' Dulac said, 'we talked, as I recall, about the vagaries of women.'

Tom didn't like to ask what these vagaries of women were. Unfortunately, Alain Dulac seemed about to elaborate anyway. He seemed to think it was quite natural to take up a conversation with a stranger where he'd left off some days before. 'What did I tell you about women?' he began.

Then Carol came into the bar. Everyone turned to look at her. Tom liked the way her blue dress matched her eyes and, of course, she had blonde hair, and she was tall and so obviously English. Tom felt pleased that he was with her.

'And this,' Dulac said, 'must be the young lady you'd lost, now found and restored to your side?'

Dulac was drunk again. He attempted to bow to Carol, but had to catch hold of the bar to stay upright. He gave Carol a wink as though his drunkenness was a great joke.

Tom could see Carol grasped the situation at once. She avoided a possible scene with a smile. He wondered where she had got this social skill and then he thought, of course she's been an air hostess. He wondered why she had given it up and turned to hairdressing. What he really wondered was why she had given up a job where she met men to work exclusively among women, but he didn't admit that to himself. Perhaps, he thought, there had been too many drunks to smile at.

'No,' Carol said to Dulac, 'I'm not that girl. I'm her friend. Show him the photo,' she said to Tom.

Tom pushed it along the bar to Dulac.

Dulac picked up the picture and narrowed his eyes to focus on it. Then he put on a pair of glasses. 'Let me see,' he said. 'You showed me another photograph of her that night. Don't you remember?'

Tom had forgotten the photo of Anna in the park that he had shown to Dulac. This one was a formal portrait of Anna sitting down. She looked very pretty, with a good figure. Dulac stared at this new photograph for a long time. 'No,' he said, 'I still don't recall seeing her.'

Tom saw the old man give Carol a look, comparing her with Anna. He wanted to tell this Frenchman with his knowing eyes that his relationship with Carol was platonic, that there was no comparison between her and Anna, but he couldn't think how you went about saying something like that.

Carol was telling Dulac. 'We've been all over looking for her,' she said. 'I was her best friend at school.'

Like someone asking tourists what sights they'd seen, Dulac demanded to know where their search had taken them. When Carol mentioned the girl at the petrol station he said he knew that place, that there was a good river for trout nearby.

Dulac, still with the photo in his hand, turned and moved unsteadily towards a group of locals sitting at a table. He was speaking in French.

'What is he saying?' Tom asked Carol.

'He says it's a photo of the missing girl.'

The men in the group studied Anna's picture.

'Fuckable,' one man said. Carol didn't translate, she assumed anyone could understand that much French.

There were two women in the group and one of them, a stocky figure, reached up and took the photo from the man. 'She's the English girl missing in the paper, isn't she? I was reading about her and her poor mother in England. It's a tragedy.' The stocky woman had been drinking.

'What's she saying?' Tom asked Carol.

'She says she's seen Anna's photo and a story in the paper about how Anna's mother is suffering.'

The stocky woman said, 'That poor mother, what she's been through with that girl. I don't know, you have your kids and you do everything you can for them, and then they break your heart.'

'What is it?' Tom asked Carol. 'What's she talking about?'

'Anna's mother,' Carol said.

The stocky woman turned to Tom. 'So you're that missing girl's sweetheart, are you?' she asked.

Carol could see the woman was the sort who got sentimental after a few drinks. 'He doesn't speak French,' Carol said. 'I'm helping him. We're retracing her steps. We think something terrible must have happened to her.'

'She didn't come here,' one of the men said. 'We notice strangers, especially if they're stacked like that one.'

'What's he saying?' Tom asked.

'He's just saying he would have remembered if he saw Anna.'

'Why's he look so happy about it?'

'He's drunk, that's all.'

'It's too early for many visitors,' Alain Dulac said, attempting to seem serious about the missing woman.

The stocky woman who had read about Mrs Turl said, 'If that girl had had an accident on the moors, Dulac would have seen her. He wouldn't miss a piece like that one. Dulac, he spends his days tramping the countryside looking for the best places to dip his rod.'

The other woman laughed. 'Oh, Jeanne,' she said. 'The things you come out with!'

'What's so funny?' Tom asked.

'Nothing,' Carol said. 'They're making fun of the fisherman.' She didn't like these crude country types. She got enough of that kind of humour at work at the hairdresser's. She was fed up with the whole boozy, sweaty side of life and she wondered if she could ever have found it amusing or colourful.

Dulac was annoyed, but he said to the woman, 'I'm here to tell you the only living thing I've seen for weeks, save sheep and rabbits and the odd deer, was a man and his woman preparing to screw behind a rock. And naturally, being a gentleman, I looked away at once.'

'You didn't question them about the girl?' the stocky woman asked. The others laughed.

'Question lovers?' Dulac said. 'I did not. If they're so carried away that he's going to hump her in the wet grass in a howling gale, I'll not interrupt such passion. Actually, she didn't look so keen on the idea. Of course, it was her little arse getting wet and scratched on the heather.'

'Where was that?' a man asked. He was an old man and looked like a farmer. Dulac explained, mentioning place names which Carol could not follow.

'That's Quimper's territory,' the old man said. 'They wouldn't get much peace if Quimper caught them screwing. If he saw them on his land he'd shoot them.'

'I've never seen this Quimper,' Dulac said, 'but I doubt it was him. From everything I've heard, he wouldn't know what to do with a woman.'

'What are they saying?' Tom asked, and Carol told him she'd tell him later. The old farmer with his leering face, so happy to talk about people fucking, upset her, and the old women were worse. Tom kept asking what they were saying.

'Who's Quimper?' Carol finally asked, so Tom would shut up. Her clear English accent startled them. They looked at each other, unsure what to say.

'He's a foreigner,' the old man said.

'I wouldn't know the man if I saw him,' one of the young men in the group said, 'but my mother used to tell me if I didn't behave that Quimper would come and take me away.'

'Quimper's crazy,' the old farmer said. 'And the crazy boy that's up there with him is as bad as he is.'

'That's his son.'

'No he isn't,' the stocky woman said. 'That's not his son. No woman would go near that one. The boy's just another crazy who hangs round there, the good God puts pigs with pigs.'

They had forgotten Tom and Carol. 'They're not saying anything, ' Carol told him in a whisper. 'They're talking about some local character, it's nothing to do with Anna.'

No one took any notice when Tom and Carol left.

'I'm sorry,' Tom said as they went down the hallway to their rooms. 'I couldn't take it, they were so damned *unconcerned* about Anna, as though her disappearing is just part of normal life.'

He was grateful for Carol's consoling hand on his arm.

'I've been so keen to question everybody, I've cheated you of dinner, haven't I? And this place is supposed to be good. At least my food guide says it is.'

'I'm not really hungry,' Carol said, lying to prevent him feeling guilty.

'Well I am,' he said. 'We'll go to my room and get room service to bring us the best thing on the menu.'

'Oh, no, you don't have to . . .'

'I insist,' Tom said. 'Don't deprive me of one small way I can say thank you for all you've done for me. For Anna, I mean. Please.'

Tom thought she was going to refuse. He hoped she wouldn't argue. He was very hungry now.

'I'd like that very much,' she said, and smiled.

He took her elbow and steered her towards his room. He was suddenly looking forward to the evening, and feeling only slightly guilty about it.

13

Toto loved games. He could imitate Quimper. It was horrible but Anna couldn't help smiling. He was a child, trying to entertain her. She couldn't reject him.

Today he was playing some new game. He was dressed as a woman. She recognized the clothes. It was one of the flashy Rosa Calvo dresses that had hung in the wardrobe in her room. He was so repellent she had to look away from him. He had red lips and he flashed his eyes in some female way he must have learned somewhere. He was disappointed she couldn't recognize who he was imitating.

'Who is it?' she asked. 'Is it Rosa Calvo?' But he ran out of the room.

When he came back the lipstick had been wiped off. He was doing someone else, another woman she didn't recognize. He drooped, he sagged. It was so forlorn it was funny. She couldn't help smiling.

'You've got me,' she said. 'Who is it?'

He laughed. Then she saw that it was herself. He was imitating her. She stopped smiling then. He began to frighten her with his play-acting. The little monster had caught her perfectly.

Toto was watching her. She smiled but then she was crying. He put his arms around her. She tried to push him away. He thought her pushing was a new game. He pinned her arms behind her back.

Then Quimper was there. He struck Toto. 'Get out of those clothes,'

Quimper snarled at him. 'We've got enough with one lady of leisure here.'

Quimper was still angry that night when he came to the room. 'Dirty whore,' he shouted at her, 'he's a retard, like a child. You won't get anywhere with him.'

Anna looked at him and she saw that he was in torment. She thought he was going to weep. He sat on the edge of the bed and forced her to kneel on the floor.

'You're too thin,' he said. He was satisfied. He'd discovered why he wasn't aroused. It was her fault. She wasn't enough of a woman for him. Even as she tried to keep herself from vomiting, she was thinking, my God, what's he going to do if I'm no use to him? He'll kill me.

She felt a kind of relief. For a second she really did. But then it started inside her, something inside her like indigestion, a burning resentment that her escape by death should be taken out of her hands. For days she'd been telling herself that one morning Quimper would come in and find her dead. Her hair kept falling out. She hadn't had a period. Each morning her gums bled bright red all over the basin as she used her finger to try to rub away the taste of Quimper. Sometimes she was so weak it was hard to stand up. And she'd greeted each of these signs as steps towards a victory, her victory over Quimper.

But if he wants me dead, she thought, then by God I'm not going to make things easy for him.

She'd seen the torment in his eyes. She jeered at him. 'I'm too thin?' she said. 'You couldn't get it up if I was Marilyn Monroe.' Marilyn Monroe was the first person who came to her mind who seemed about the right period for him.

Quimper got up and left the room.

It was a kind of victory. She was thinking about that next day, alone in the kitchen gazing out of the window taking in the heart-breaking signs of spring. She imagined how Godlingford would be looking in the sunshine. She imagined Tom in Godlingford and her eyes blurred.

She blinked. There was someone there. A tall man was standing among the boulders staring at the house.

She thought, I'm hallucinating. My eyes are playing tricks.

But he was there.

She tried to reach the window but the chain was too short, She couldn't reach it.

Let him see me, she prayed, I'll do anything you want me to do if you'll only let me out of here.

And all the while the man didn't move but stood gazing at the house.

In the yard the dog began to bark. The man turned. He was carrying a fishing box and rod, and he walked away across the rock-strewn moor towards the woods. She watched as he gradually disappeared into the new green leaves of the trees.

She didn't know how long she stared at the place where he'd stood. The line of sodden gorse and grey boulders lay uninterrupted against a grey sky. Then she saw Quimper walking slowly down the track to where the man had been standing. Quimper was carrying a shotgun over the crook of his arm.

She turned away from the window. Quimper mustn't see her watching. She sat at the kitchen table with her back to the window. After a little while Quimper and Toto were by the back door. 'He's gone,' she heard Quimper say.

'Who was it?' Toto asked.

'A fisherman,' Quimper said. 'Probably a lost tourist looking for somewhere to fish.'

'You think he'll come back?' Toto asked, but Quimper said nothing she could hear.

He'd gone. It was an accident, a fisherman strayed from some path he hoped would lead to a river or a lake. Was he even staring at the farm, not just looking beyond the buildings at the mountains behind? There was no reason why he should come back again.

She tried not to think about it until she was on her own. Then she lay in the dark and let herself hope. There was still a world out there with people in it. People did come to this Godforsaken place. There'd been the man in the distance and now the fisherman. Twice, and both times she'd failed to make contact.

In the cold darkness then she came as near as she ever did to real despair. It wasn't like the hours she'd spent in this house full of dread and self recrimination about being parted from Tom and a life she loved and wanted back. That was horrible and frightening and after she'd cried herself out she felt numb. The despair she felt now was different. It had nothing to do with losing hope or any other kind of feeling. The terrible thing about it was that it was logical. It was a mental thing, a fact. Nothing she could do would change it.

Funny that it was Nick Gold, of all people, who came to her rescue then. Nick who was quite simply a despicable human being except he was her boss and had created the firm where she earned her living. But that's the way it was, she suddenly heard Nick Gold's voice in her head as she'd heard it on the telephone across the months she'd known him, 'Don't fight 'em, fuck 'em'.

She'd never even thought about what he'd meant, it was just what he always said when something went wrong and there was nothing he could do about it. Now, Anna thought, I can't change what's happened. There's not going to be a miracle rescue. I've got to accept it. I've got to put everything else behind me and see that it's no good dreaming of going back. This is my life now. I can only go forward from here.

14

Alain Dulac was drunk but no more drunk than usual. 'I tell you,' he said, 'I saw a woman there.'

'You're seeing things, my friend,' Herbert Baubel, the policeman, told him. 'I don't come here after a hard day's detective work to hear fairy stories.' They were in the bar overlooking the square in Goriac. Baubel was off duty.

'I wasn't drunk,' Dulac said. 'She was at the window.'

But he wasn't sure what he'd seen. However, if there was something wrong at Quimper's he didn't want to be blamed later on for not telling what he saw. He had, in fact, been drinking when he saw her. There'd been no fish, he'd finished his flask to keep warm.

Baubel wanted to amuse himself with a few drinks. 'Maybe it was a ghost you saw,' he said.

Dulac shrugged. Abstracted, he stared through the window at the town square. It was market day but now the stallholders were packing up to leave, making much noise, taking down the awnings and dismantling the trestles. It's true, he thought, it was only an impression of a woman, it was something like seeing a ghost. When he returned from his fruitless day's fishing, he came into the bar to consider if he should tell anyone. Then Baubel came in and now, he told himself, his duty was done.

Baubel raised his glass. '*Santé*,' he said.

Dulac raised his eyes and met Baubel's brown stare. 'Maybe you're right,' Dulac said, 'but I keep thinking about that young couple looking for the missing English girl.'

'What young couple?' Baubel asked.

'You weren't there that night. It was the Englishman from Surrey with the lost fiancée.'

'Goddam Godlingford,' Baubel said in English. 'I know all about him, as if I wouldn't with the English police on the telephone every other day asking for a "progress report".'

'The Englishman was here last weekend making a search for himself. He said some unflattering things about the police. He had a nice English blonde with him. She spoke French, she said she was a friend of the missing girl.'

'Do you think he did away with her?' Baubel asked. 'He could have done it. We found nothing to suggest she ever came here. It could be a plot to cover his tracks. He brings his mistress here to help him look for the disappeared woman, and all the while that poor girl is rotting away under his newly laid patio paving in a nice English suburb.'

'Well,' Dulac said, 'perhaps you have a true insight into the criminal mind. But it would be the end of all your chances for promotion out of here if that was the missing Englishwoman I saw at Quimper's window.'

'If you were so bothered,' Baubel said, 'why didn't you go and get a better look?'

'My days of heroics are over,' Dulac said.

Baubel knew this was a reference to Dulac's days in the Resistance. In spite of his drinking he was a trim, spare man, in wonderful condition for his years. He'd been a hero in the War.

'The dog was raging,' Dulac said. 'And Quimper came out with a shotgun. He doesn't like trespassers.'

'They say that boy of his is back from the coast. Did you see anything of him? You'd have something in common with him. He's a fisherman, too.'

'That's not fishing, that's fish-harvesting. I didn't want Quimper to see me. There's a little spot I've been fishing on his land, and I don't want him looking out for me.'

'You mean you're poaching?'

'I didn't catch anything. Are you poaching when you're trying to catch a fish, or do you have to land one to qualify? All I'm saying is, I wouldn't give much for your chances of being promoted out of this backwater if they find that girl dead at Quimper's and it transpires you didn't check out a sighting.'

'What sighting?'

'My sighting. I saw a woman there.'

Baubel gave a contemptuous snort. 'It seems much more likely she went off with another man. The English police have discovered her character. She has a past. At least, she's a very modern young woman.'

'Modern women,' Dulac said. 'even in the old days there were plenty of *modern* women.'

He said this as a joke but there was a bitter tone to his voice. Baubel had been only three years in this Brittany backwater. He did not know the full story of Alain Dulac except that he had been a hero in the Resistance; now, he thought, he perhaps should add that Alain Dulac was also a man who had been let down by a woman and was still bitter about it.

The two men drank in silence, then Baubel said, 'I suppose there's no harm in going up there to have a look.'

'No harm at all, I'd say. It would leave you in the clear.'

'No need to call out the troops. A routine inquiry, just being thorough,' Baubel said, as much to himself as to Dulac.

'I'd say so.'

'Tomorrow, then. I'll go up there tomorrow.'

'Why not now?' Dulac said. 'I'll come with you.'

Baubel looked at the level of the pastis in the Ricard bottle behind the bar. He shook his head. 'I'm off duty now,' he said. 'First thing in the morning. You can show me where you saw your vision.'

Dulac was sober and hungover. He had not even had time for one glass of something curative that morning. He wished he had not come. He wished he had never mentioned the woman he thought he might have seen. The state of the tarmac road was bad enough, the way he felt, but when Baubel, who was only a provincial ass of a policeman and couldn't even drive properly, turned the car off and started up the long rough track to Quimper's farm, Dulac was certain he was about to die. The car roared and groaned and grated on the stony ruts. He looked at Baubel and decided that the policeman wasn't even dressed to drive in this terrain; Baubel's uniform jacket was so tight that he could scarcely move his arms. He's like a cop in a comic cartoon, Dulac thought.

'This Quimper must be a madman,' Dulac said. 'How can he tolerate this trip all the time?'

'His name's Rostov. He's from the Ukraine,' Baubel said, as if that explained the rough road. 'He only comes out once a month for provisions. He doesn't like visitors. This way he can see them coming a mile off. He can't be taken by surprise.'

Baubel was red in the face. He tried to avoid a pothole and in doing so he stalled the car. 'This is a waste of time. We're not slipping in to surprise him,' he said, 'the old villain will be waiting for us when we get there.'

'We should have come last night, on foot,' Dulac said.

'You weren't all that steady on your feet last night, my friend,' Baubel said.

As they approached the final steep slope that led to the farm, Dulac thought they could be stepping back centuries. The gabled blue-grey stone house, with a slate roof stained red with lichen, the protecting yard of stone barns and byres, it looked like a place out of ancient,

98

more dangerous, times, as if it were expecting a raid from a marauding band. Those times didn't seem far removed to Dulac. He liked thinking about them. Sometimes when he was fishing, or out walking alone in the mountains, he thought he could feel the spirit of the mythic Breton knight who shared his name. During the War he had learned that the English claimed the same legend. He and a British agent had argued about it. They had enjoyed themselves very much and the War had seemed a long way off.

Maybe I am after all just an old man who is seeing things, he said to himself. Maybe it was Morgana la Fey I saw at the window. Or the enchantress, Viviane, who cast a spell on Merlin and imprisoned him in the castle.

'There's something sinister about this place,' Dulac said. 'Where is everybody?'

Two rounded ricks, hay or straw, their humped backsides bleached by the wind and streaked with black by the driving rain, offered the only sign that a human hand was active here. A large dung heap inside the wall of the yard proved there were animals hidden somewhere. Scrawny chickens scratched for worms in the manure. And, as they drove through the gate into the yard, a dog began to bark.

'What did I tell you?' Baubel said. 'Nobody can sneak up on this place. If Quimper has put in a new patio we'll dig it up.'

Baubel laughed at his own joke, but Dulac didn't think it was anything to laugh at.

'Here's the ogre now,' Baubel said.

Quimper stepped out from the shadow of the stone barn and came towards them before Baubel stopped the car.

'Good morning,' Baubel said through his open window. Then he turned to Dulac. 'Look at him,' he said, 'a specimen of one of the larger apes.'

The two men climbed stiffly out of the car. Dulac, stretching gingerly, tested each arm and leg for damage. 'My God,' he said, 'they should use that road of yours to test army tanks.'

Baubel walked up to Quimper, who was standing perfectly still, like a beast, Dulac thought, and Baubel picked up Quimper's right hand as if it were an inanimate object and shook it up and down. Quimper seemed as if he failed to notice. 'This is Alain Dulac,' Baubel said.

'Yes?' Quimper said.

Dulac, standing to one side, wondered if Quimper recognized him as the man he'd seen watching the house. Dulac tried to see if the fellow was reacting to the sight of him. But from the tall Dulac's height all he could see of Quimper's expression was the bristling outcrop of dark eyebrows. He's an old peasant from far away in the east, Dulac thought.

Suddenly Quimper came to life. 'Is this an official visit?' he asked.

He doesn't betray much, Dulac thought, he's a real foreigner. Only there was something about the way he stood, foursquare like one of the squat flat-topped boulders strewn over his land, which made it clear he was not pleased to see them. But then everyone said he was a hermit, never pleased to see people.

'Just routine,' Baubel said. 'Officially we're looking for a woman, a young Englishwoman who went missing. You'll have read about it? Or seen the posters?'

'No,' Quimper said. He shrugged. Dulac saw that the man's shoulders were powerful, toned by the heavy work of the farm.

'Well,' Baubel said, 'we are looking for her. We've got to cover every possibility.'

Quimper pointed at Dulac. 'Who is he?' he asked. 'Is he a flic?'

'No,' Baubel said. He almost laughed at the idea. 'He's helping with the search. He thinks he may have seen a woman looking out of a window here the other day.'

'Oh, he did, did he?' Quimper said. 'And what was he doing snooping round on my private property? And if he saw a woman, what's that supposed to signify? It's not against the law for a man to have a woman in his house, is it?'

He turned his head and fixed Dulac with a look. He's something out of Dostoevsky, Dulac, who once read books, said to himself. Not a main character but a minor figure whom someone mistreated when he was a boy and who now beats his wife and children in return.

Baubel spoke very carefully to Quimper, slowly, as though he was trying to keep his temper with an imbecile. 'No, it's not illegal. But it would be unusual in this house, wouldn't it? As I said, we have to check everything because of the missing Englishwoman.'

'I won't be spied on,' Quimper said. 'You've no right.'

'We don't spy, *monsieur*. But the rumour is you are very much a bachelor. So, we check.'

'So?' Quimper said. 'You think I have a woman imprisoned here? Come with me.' Dulac watched Quimper's lips folding back, like a dog preparing to bite. That's what a specimen like that does for a smile, Dulac told himself. Quimper turned and led them to the back door of the house. 'You will see the tragedy of a man who is misunderstood,' he said. 'You'll see one of my many tragedies.'

What's he talking about now? Dulac thought. He's whingeing, like a character in Dostoevsky whinges, despairing of his fate as he puts his daughter out on the street to be a whore. They followed Quimper into the house across the dark stone-flagged kitchen, and then up narrow stairs leading to a long corridor. At one door Quimper paused, listening. Then he threw the door open and Baubel and Dulac followed him into a square room, sparsely furnished with a single bed, a dressing-table and an open wardrobe in which they saw women's clothes. The wallpaper was yellow with faded blue flowers. It smelled of damp but the window, shaded by half-open shutters, was open and looked out across the open moor towards woods in the distance. It was a pretty view.

There was a pile of women's clothes on the bed. Baubel had a teenage daughter and he thought this room looked like hers after she had been deciding what to wear to go out. There was a pair of high-heeled shoes on the floor. They were a large size, Baubel thought, larger than his daughter's. The room stank of scent as well as damp.

'You see?' Dulac said in a loud whisper to Baubel, 'What did I tell you? There is a woman here.'

Then the door behind them opened and a woman came into the room. She was a bizarre sight. Her heavy make-up was smudged as though she had just returned from a drunken party. She had long red hair which she started brushing with a dreamy imbecile expression on her face.

'You see?' Quimper said. 'Now do you see?' He was quite angry, as if they were seeing something he didn't want them to see.

Baubel saw that it wasn't a young woman.

Dulac cleared his throat looking at the young man in women's clothes. Even Baubel was embarrassed, he looked at his feet.

'This is what you saw,' Quimper said to Dulac. 'When he thinks I'm out, he dresses like this. Do you want him to walk about and swing his hips for you?'

The poor boy's not all there, Dulac thought, he shouldn't be made fun of like this. But the stink of the perfume was overwhelming. Dulac lit a cigarette and went and stood by the window. He pushed back the shutters for a wider view.

'That's your young woman,' Quimper said. 'You can add that to the list, can't you?'

'What list is that?' Baubel asked. They were following Quimper out of the room and back down the stairs.

'The list of the things they say against crazy Quimper. You know how they are, the people here. They think I'm crazy.' He turned to confront them. 'You tell me,' he said, 'what can I do? It's the way he is. I've tried to get him interested in women, but he prefers this play-acting.'

'He's your son?' Baubel asked.

'He's no son of mine,' Quimper said. 'But I took him in. I felt sorry for him. I have no one else to help with the farm. He's a good worker when he wants to be.'

Baubel attempted to look sympathetic. 'It's a large world, *monsieur*, with many things in it. One must be tolerant.'

'If he was different he could find a woman. Then she could have a child and I'd leave the place to him when I go. I would. I'd do that.'

'What about you?' Baubel asked. 'You could find a woman.'

'It's too late for that, I'm too old,' Quimper said.

He looked strong as a bull to Baubel but one never knew when the desire left a man. Baubel couldn't see Quimper kidnapping the English girl and imagining that she would produce an heir with the half-wit.

They left Quimper standing in the yard. As they drove down the track he kept standing there, staring them off the premises. Then when Dulac looked back again Quimper was gone. Dulac saw the shutters of the window in the room being closed.

'I've heard of such things, of course,' Dulac said. 'But in Paris.'

Baubel smiled. In Brittany they had all heard of everything, but always in Paris. Baubel became philosophic. 'Quimper has never been loved,' he said, 'and he is not even liked. I can understand, but he is a sad case just the same.'

'Of course,' Baubel said, 'Quimper is sick in the head, he has persecution mania.' Baubel sighed. 'And as for the boy, Toto, that's a tragedy.'

'Do you think he is his son?'

'Who knows? He says no. Or he said, "He's no son of mine", which is a thing fathers say.'

'What happened to the mother then?' Dulac asked.

Baubel shrugged. 'God only knows. Toto suddenly appeared. No one knows where he came from. Maybe it's as Quimper says and the kid simply arrived one day.'

'I can't see Quimper doing charity work, taking in the boy,' Dulac said.

103

'Maybe he was lonely.'

'Maybe he was lonely enough to kidnap the English girl for company?' Dulac said.

There was a short silence. Baubel knew how lonely Dulac must be himself. Baubel was driving too fast. The car bucked over the ruts.

'You saw your *girl* in the window,' Baubel said.

'I suppose so,' Dulac said. 'But there's one thing.'

'What thing?'

'The hair. She didn't have red hair. The one I saw had dark hair.'

Baubel laughed. 'I suppose a man like you wouldn't know but women change their hair with their outfits these days. They wear wigs.'

'Does the name Rosa Calvo mean anything to you?' Dulac said.

'Rosa Calvo? A film star, perhaps? Why do you ask?' He thought the old man was getting peculiar.

'Just a name that's fixed in my mind,' Dulac said. He had seen that name carved in the windowsill. And there's something else, he thought, that window had been nailed down for years. He saw the fresh splintered marks in the wood where someone had pulled out the nails in a hell of a hurry. Probably they had been taken out that very day, there were tiny slivers of wood still there where the nails had been pulled out. The way the wind blew out here on the moors they wouldn't be there tomorrow. Why should anyone un-nail them in such a hurry? Perhaps it rattles in the winter, he thought. The winds were fierce in winter, across that open moor. But the face of that creature in the house was moronic, it wasn't the face I saw, or the face I thought I saw, in the window. 'He could have kidnapped the English girl,' Dulac said.

'Why?' Baubel said, 'to do the housework?'

'To look at,' Dulac said. 'She was pretty. In the picture in the paper she was very pretty.'

Baubel knew that Dulac was once married to a pretty woman. She had run off and left him for a chemist. Ever since, Dulac had lived alone. When a man lived alone for thirty years he gets strange ideas,

Baubel thought. But it wasn't only living alone that could give a man strange ideas. Brittany was a haunted place. It seemed to Baubel that anyone who spent more than five years or so in this barbaric place was touched in the head. He himself had come here only three years ago, from Normandy, which was a place of culture and reason. He was sorry now to see that Dulac, who came here from Provence many years ago, seemed to have become as crazy as the natives.

15

Since Anna had disappeared there had been so many hurtful stories about her in the newspapers that Tom had stopped looking at them, even the *Daily Telegraph*. As for the tabloids, they told such lies. But there was no escaping them. He was at his desk at the bank and someone had left a copy of the gutter press there. From where he was sitting he could see a photo of Anna. It wasn't the Anna he knew. She had bleached blonde hair, and she was wearing a shiny black plastic skirt, sitting on a motorbike looking tough. The idea, of course, was that a girl like that was bound to go missing, bound, even, to get herself murdered. The newspapers had plainly persuaded Mrs Turl, who was quoted by one and all as the heroic grieving mother prepared to sacrifice her errant daughter's guilty secrets to recover her from a fate worse than death, that publicity was her most powerful weapon in tracing Anna. The woman was also making money from her lies. Tom felt unkind in thinking this, but it was obvious. The tabloids, without new pictures of Anna, photographed Mrs Turl. Even Tom could see how the process of her grief was clearly reflected in her increasingly expensive *coiffures* and designer clothes.

Most of all, though, Tom resented the sanctimonious tone the newspapers used about Anna. Their hypocrisy made him furious. He felt like complaining to the Press Council, he felt like suing the newspapers; he even had visions of seeking out the men who wrote the stories and knocking them down. And for him there was something worse than the way they treated Anna as a lost soul for whom they sought salvation.

They had got hold of a photo of him.

He didn't know how they had got it. Someone must have taken it as he came out of the bank after work one day. The tabloid that printed it first put it alongside a picture of Anna at sixteen. Tom had torn the paper into small pieces, but the caption remained to haunt him. 'SUGAR DADDY GOOD-TIME GIRL ANNA FLED.' Tom could see that for anyone who didn't know that the photo of Anna had been taken years ago, there was indeed something perverted about the sad middle-aged man being engaged to that girl. And though Tom had always refused to talk to the reporters, they quoted him anyway, saying, 'I don't care what Anna's done, I want her back.'

It was a nightmare. He'd never said that. He never would say that. They had no right to put words into his mouth like that. They were messing with things he hadn't even worked out in his own mind.

He tried to ask himself why he minded so much that they had quoted things he'd never said or thought. It was simply a tabloid formula. Some people would probably tell him to forget it, it didn't matter, nobody took what that kind of newspaper said seriously. But, he told himself, the powers-that-be in the bank might. Mr Tetley hadn't actually said anything specific. Whenever he couldn't avoid speaking to Tom, he'd ask about Anna as 'your unfortunate fiancée' or something equally impersonal. Mr Tetley was embarrassed, certainly, but that embarrassment showed signs of becoming annoyance. Clearly Mr Tetley wanted Tom to disavow any current or future connection with Anna Turl.

It was first thing in the morning. Tom was alone in the bank. Someone had left another newspaper on his desk last night so he'd see it this morning. They were laughing at him. When Anna came back from wherever she'd gone they'd laugh in front of him and not merely behind his back as they were doing now.

He threw the newspaper into the waste bin without looking at it. Then he switched on the percolator to reheat the dregs of yesterday's coffee. He'd come in early because he couldn't sleep. At home he'd have to face his mother fussing over him. The atmosphere between them was heavy with her disapproval of Anna, though she couldn't say anything because the girl might have been murdered.

I've got to think, he told himself. What do I think? Why do I mind that quote they made up so much? And there came a sneaky answering whisper in his head, Why should you mind if it's true? So isn't it true?

His head started to throb. He had to work this out for himself. He had to know what he really felt about Anna now. But it was too hard. What did other people do when they had to face something like this? He couldn't ask for counselling, he wasn't that kind of person. But he wanted to talk to someone. Suddenly he felt bereft that he had no friend or relative he could talk to. It was ridiculous. He knew lots of people at the sports club. There were people at work. He spent time with them, but they talked about rugby and work. And then there had always been Anna.

But he couldn't talk about this to Anna. Not only literally, he couldn't even if she weren't missing. He couldn't reveal to her that he'd doubted her. She would never understand what had happened to him since she disappeared.

For a moment, he went cold with fear at the thought of facing Anna again now. He didn't know what they could say to each other, and the thought of the silence there would be between them terrified him. Whatever had happened to her, he realized that she would not be able to make him understand. He had no imagination, he knew that. But it wasn't only that. It had been a revelation to him to discover that he didn't know, he had never known, who or what she was really. He had thought he knew his Anna, but now he knew that his Anna was only a fragment of the whole person.

He didn't blame her. She hadn't lied to him deliberately. It was his fault, probably, that their relationship had never scratched deeper beneath the surface of either him or her. Intimacy meant that they slept together. He hadn't realized that there was more to it than that.

Tom drank the rest of the coffee, which had stewed and now gone cold again. He thought, I found it easier to talk to that friend of hers when we were in France than I did to Anna. Really talk.

Carol, that was who he had to talk to. It was suddenly so obvious, he could scarcely stop himself grabbing the phone and ringing her now. But it was too early. He only had her work number to hand.

As he wondered how soon she was likely to get to the hairdressing salon so he could ring her, the telephone on his desk rang. He decided not to answer it. Bank customers should ring in office hours. But he couldn't ignore it, he never had been able to. It drove him mad in television dramas when people didn't answer a ringing phone.

'Mr Pritchard?' Tom recognized the voice of Inspector Parrish.

A body had been found. Tom was glad he was sitting down.

'A young woman's body,' Parrish said, 'on a golf course outside Guildford.' Then he paused. 'For various reasons,' he said, 'identification is difficult. We can't say it's Miss Turl. On the other hand, we can't say it isn't.'

Tom was leaving to meet the police car when Duffy came in, looking pleased with himself. Then he remembered that Tom was in trouble and he acquired a sympathetic look. 'How are you?' Duffy asked. Tom told him about the body on the golf course. He watched Duffy's reaction and thought he saw it suddenly occur to Duffy that Tom could be a suspect. Inspector Parrish must think the same thing, Tom told himself. This nightmare got worse and worse. He thought, where was I the day Anna disappeared? At home. Mother was there. I went out jogging. I didn't see anyone. No one saw me. I've read about cases like that, and it's always said that the man obviously did it. In crimes of passion the killer doesn't stop to give himself an alibi.

'Look,' Duffy said, 'would you like me to come with you? I mean, it's an awful thing to have to do alone.'

Tom had not expected this. He had been thinking Duffy thought he was a murderer and here was this sudden kindness. Tom felt as though he had tears in his eyes. He lowered his head so that Duffy wouldn't see them if they were actually there. 'That's very good of you, Duffy,' he said. 'I appreciate it. But I'm better on my own.'

On an impulse, he grabbed Duffy's hand and shook it. Duffy looked surprised but he squeezed Tom's hand. 'Good luck,' he said, and then he was embarrassed.

'See you later,' Tom said as he hurried out.

Inspector Parrish was waiting outside the bank and as they drove along Tom found himself thinking that it would be Anna's body and that at last he'd know what had happened to her, that she hadn't run away, that he could now mourn her as another victim of a hideous urban society. Still, it wouldn't end there. He was the chief suspect. They'd ask how he and Anna had been getting on, had they quarrelled? They would start digging into their relationship, into his life, sorry for him at first because he was feeble and couldn't get himself a better alibi. Then they would become determined, believing him guilty. Tom knew he wasn't guilty, but he looked as if he were. He felt guilty. He dreaded their questions. He was ashamed of his life. He couldn't explain even to himself why this should be so, but it was. He did his best at work, he looked after his mother; he won trophies for sport, he loved Anna. It wasn't enough: he was ashamed of that.

'You all right?' Inspector Parrish asked.

Tom nodded, trying to smile.

When they got there he was nauseated. He kept his eyes on the floor.

'It'll soon be over,' Inspector Parrish said.

The body wasn't Anna's. How could he ever have thought it would be? Anna wasn't going to get herself murdered. Tom stared down at the young female body on the slab. He was embarrassed to see her like that, as she would never allow him to look at her if she'd been alive. It under-lined how absent life was. Tom tried to imagine what the woman would have looked like before the ... He didn't know what to call it. Inspector Parrish said there had been interference with a blunt instrument. Such an odd expression, but what would you call what had happened to the woman? Tom suddenly thought, What will Anna look like when it's her corpse I have to look at?

He turned away. 'How could anyone do that?' he asked. 'Who'd do a thing like that?'

'Probably someone you wouldn't expect,' Inspector Parrish said. 'Probably someone very quiet whom no one would ever suspect, until she's identified and we find out who her friends were.'

Someone very quiet. Tom felt dizzy. Inspector Parrish took his arm. 'Sorry about that,' Inspector Parrish said as they went out of the room.

In the car back to Godlingford, Tom had to ask Inspector Parrish to pull to the side of the road. He got out and vomited. When he got back in he apologized.

'If it's no trouble,' Tom said, 'can you drop me off at Anna's mother's place. It's not out of your way.'

If Inspector Parrish was surprised, he didn't show it. 'I just thought,' Tom explained, 'Mrs Turl might hear about a woman being found. She might read it in the papers and think it was Anna.'

'I've got an idea the Guildford police will be asking Mrs Turl to have a look at that body,' Inspector Parrish said.

'Good God,' Tom said, 'whatever for?'

Then, as soon as he said it, he knew the reason. They wanted to double check. Of course they would. If Tom failed to identify the body and then Mrs Turl said it was Anna, they'd have him. That's how their minds worked.

Inspector Parrish gave Tom a curious look. Tom almost said, 'You look as though you think I killed Anna', but then he thought better of it. Keep your mouth shut, he told himself. This is serious, they're probably in there now at the bank checking the books to see if I've been stealing money.

When they stopped outside Mrs Turl's house, the inspector said, 'Do you want me to wait? I'll come with you if it helps.'

Tom refused the offer. He wondered if he looked odd in some way, first Duffy and now Inspector Parrish offering to accompany him on unpleasant errands.

He walked up to the front door and rang the bell. He listened to the opening bars of 'Land of Hope and Glory' four times over before he accepted that Mrs Turl was not at home. Then he noticed a message propped against a collection of dirty empty milk bottles. 'Press call. Back later.'

Oh God, Tom thought, what was she up to now. He'd hoped the newspapers might lose interest in the story so that he could start reading them again without dreading what he was going to see. He thought, if only Anna's mother would keep her mouth shout, but then he told himself he wasn't being fair. The poor wretched woman must think she was helping Anna by keeping the story going, that someone somewhere would remember something . . . and maybe she was right.

16

Anna had known something out of the ordinary was happening because Quimper suddenly appeared in the kitchen in the middle of the day. He seemed to be in a great hurry. He was sweating and breathing heavily. He bound her hands and feet with twine and forced his filthy handkerchief into her mouth as a gag. He unchained her. Then he blindfolded her.

She felt herself being dragged across the stone floor. She heard him open a door, and then she was bumping against stone as he pulled her down the steps to the cellar. Then he dropped her and she heard his boots going up the stairs. A door slammed and she heard the sound of a bolt slammed shut.

She strained her ears but she could hear only the drip of water on the stone floor. Then somewhere close there was a different dripping into deep water. The two notes made a syncopated beat in her head. Gradually there were other sounds, a curious rustling she couldn't understand until she felt something scuttle across her calves. It was the rasping of the horny bodies of beetles.

Then came a ringing of boots above her head, not Quimper's footsteps. Not Toto's, either. She tried to open her mouth, but the gag was too tight. She couldn't scream. She tried to thump her feet on the floor, but she couldn't make any noise at all against the thick stone. The footsteps went away. That was it.

It seemed like hours before she heard the bolt drawn back and Quimper's footsteps.

'All right, it's over. Get back upstairs now,' he said. He used a knife to cut through the twine and the handkerchief. She tried to stand up, but her legs gave way. He pulled her to her feet and pushed her ahead of him up the stone steps to the kitchen.

There everything seemed as it had been before. Toto was there, that was all. Quimper fastened the shackle round her ankle.

'I did good,' Toto said.

'Yes,' Quimper said, 'but now you'll have to make yourself scarce.'

Quimper sounded weary.

'I won't go,' Toto said. He jumped to his feet, his face an angry red that clashed with his hair. 'I want to stay,' he screamed.

'You're stupid,' Quimper shouted at him. 'You don't know what they do to people like you.'

It struck Anna that Quimper was offended. He was disgusted. He couldn't look at Toto. He turned away from him and his eyes rested on her. It was almost as though he was looking to her as if she was his wife and should tell him how to cope with a boy like Toto.

'What happened?' she asked.

'Nothing to do with you,' Quimper said.

But something was disturbing him.

'You should have seen yourself,' Quimper said to Toto. 'It was disgusting, making eyes like a whore. Where did you learn such things? They'll come back and lock you up.'

She didn't know what they were talking about. All at once she felt she was going to faint. 'Water,' she said.

Toto looked at Quimper. He seemed glad of the distraction.

'Give her a glass of wine,' Quimper said.

The wine tasted sour.

She didn't feel faint because of weakness from hours lying in the cellar, or even out of delayed phobia about creepy-crawlies. What made it seem as though all the blood had drained out of her head was the sudden realization that something tremendous had happened.

There had been outsiders in the house, visitors who had seen Toto doing one of his pantomime dame acts.

And, she thought, if strangers were in the house, outsiders who had braved Quimper to come here, they must have been looking for me. The tall fisherman saw me. He must have done. He must have come looking for me.

Somehow Quimper had had enough time to dress Toto as a woman to fool anyone who came because the fisherman had sighted her. Toto must have got carried away with the part. He was a child, and Quimper had obviously been shocked by his performance. She'd have been pleased at that if it didn't mean that the wretched boy had obviously put her would-be rescuers off the scent. Damn Toto.

But even so she was excited. It made her reckless.

'You want to be careful,' she said to Toto, 'they'll think Quimper is a pervert living here with you. They'll come and take him away.'

She thought Quimper was going to hit her.

'Shut your mouth, bitch,' he snarled. 'I do the talking here; keep that dog's mouth of yours shut. But she's right,' he said to Toto. 'You've got to get out of here. You'd better go back to the coast.'

Toto's face was drawn. He didn't want to leave Quimper. Anna couldn't understand why, but he loved Quimper. Toto looked at the man as if accepting fatherly advice. 'It'll pass,' Quimper said. 'Then you can return.'

Toto looked at her as though he wanted her help but she could think of nothing to say. She sat unable to move.

She had no idea what time it was. She could have been in the cellar for hours, or much less. Quimper took her upstairs and locked her into her room.

A faint odour of Gitanes lingered in the air. The nails in the window had been removed and then banged back in. Anna wondered if, now they'd been loosened, she might be able to work them out of the wood.

She couldn't sleep. In her head she went over and over what had happened. She asked herself again and again what she could have done to alert the strangers to her presence. She thought, it isn't possible that I could've been under their noses and not exist to them. They were looking for me, for God's sake, and I had left no trace. They've gone.

She waited for the familiar onrush of despair, almost like an old friend, but this time it did not come. Instead she felt a growing swell of anger. She was angry with herself, and with Toto, but most of all she was angry with those gullible strangers who hadn't made more effort not to be fooled by Quimper and the dim-witted Toto. Having her hopes raised and then dashed was too much. Damn you, God, she thought, you fucking sadist, this isn't fair.

17

Alain Dulac woke from a horrible dream of long red hair, thick red hair growing six or eight metres long. He had dreamed that they had opened his wife's grave and it was full of her auburn hair which had never stopped growing. His wife's corpse had said something to him in the dream, he couldn't remember what, something cruel. She still hated him. The boy at Quimper's house had red hair. Dreams were very strange, the stranger the older he got.

The sun was shining but he was in no hurry to go out. Each morning he took pleasure in the slow deliberate action of a man with nothing to do, of a man without wife or children or a job to rush to. He heard the wind rustling the skeleton of the creeper outside his window. It was the only sound. It's good drinking weather, he thought, a nice fresh chill in the air. But today, before any drinking, there was something he must do first.

Damn that lad and his red hair. It was ridiculous of course, but the red wig had stirred memories. It was a ghastly dream. Her red hair had filled the coffin. When the box was opened yards and yards of flame-red hair had spilled out of it. Dulac didn't want to think of his wife, of how different his days had been when she was with him in Provence. He didn't know if she was dead with her red hair still growing in the coffin. She could still be alive for all he knew.

He had got used to being alone when he was living with her, and now he'd got used to it all over again. There were days and days when he saw no one unless he went into the village for a drink. He looked around the room, it was so familiar that he didn't even recognize it any more, and he thought how no woman had ever been inside this room, not even to clean, not since he had come to Brittany all those years ago to get away from her and the memories that had haunted the old house outside Uzès where they'd lived. She hated that house. At least, after she became bored with him, she used to say she hated it; and then, after a while, she said she hated him as well. There was another man, naturally there was. Dulac's wife had learned to hate him so much that she told him about the other man after only a month of pretending there was no one else. She went to live with the man, a chemist in Uzès. After that Dulac couldn't go into Uzès to buy anything without thinking he saw her. It was hell. He had to move. He had moved, but still she could come back like a ghost to him in his dreams, a pest to him even when she was dead in her coffin, like last night. It was absurd that a ridiculous boy could bring her back. When he'd looked at the boy the dirty little devil had caught something in Dulac's eye and winked at him. It was humiliating. Of course the boy didn't know what he was doing. He was backward, a dimwit who liked dressing-up as a child might.

Where had he got those clothes? They were theatrical, like a gypsy's costume. Certainly they weren't the sort of clothes an Englishwoman would wear except at a fancy dress party.

Then Dulac began thinking of his wife again. Her hair wouldn't be red any more. She'd be grey by now. Perhaps she was dead. Dead or alive, she'd be ugly at last. The wife of a provincial chemist.

'To hell with it,' he said aloud. 'I need a new gaff anyway. I'll take myself to town to get it. And I'll do this other thing while I'm at it.'

Two hours later, after only one restorative stop, he dismounted from his bicycle outside the library in Goriac. Inside, a kindly, middle-aged woman showed him how to use the microfiche. He could tell it made her feel modern, showing an old boy how the thing ticked. When he got it working, the slabs of print, shimmering slightly, appeared on the screen, and he thought the old newspapers cheated decay with this, technology saving them from the oblivion he would soon be going to. The human dead, they were gone for ever. In his mind he'd killed his wife off while he rode his bicycle here. Then it had broken his heart to think of her as dead, but it was better, he thought, than seeing her alive with the provincial chemist. He had decided over the only cognac of the morning that she was dead and that she had died young, while her hair was still red and before the chemist could enjoy her too much. It was a pleasant thought, denying the chemist long lusty years in the matrimonial bed. The thought comforted Dulac, although the idea of her old and worn out, with none of her beauty remaining and, of course, the chemist hating her and her hating the chemist, was also pleasing. Now, seated in the library before the magic-seeming machine, he thought that perhaps he might bring her back to life and have the two of them, her and the chemist, wear themselves out with bickering.

He shook her from his mind. There was that other woman, Rosa Calvo. Was she also one of the dead? The name, an unusual name, had been troubling him since he saw it carved into the windowsill. He put on his half-frame reading and fly-tieing glasses and bent forward to peer at the screen. What a lot of useless words there were in newspapers, he thought, as page after page of nonsense unscrolled. It was surprising how much the local newspaper had changed over the years. He hadn't noticed. It was the advertisements. There were so many more of them, for cars and weekend cottages and jobs in the tourist hotels. When he'd come to Brittany the paper had been full of advertisements for livestock and farm implements; Brittany was real country then, country that had won him over because it was like stepping back in time, into a past that did not contain painful memories for him. The bleak, rocky, rainswept landscape was in sympathy with his feelings. He'd been a fool. He smiled at his stupidity. He should have stayed in the warm South, it was

121

kinder to old bones. To hell with the chemists of Uzès and whatever women they happened to have.

He read slowly. He tried not to, but he kept getting caught up in the local dramas of the past. It is, after all, my own lifetime, he told himself, times I have lived through. They seemed boring, of no importance whatsoever. He thought that perhaps in the end the life he lived in his head, full of the tragi-comedy of red-headed women and chemists, was the only real, important and exciting thing in his life, at least since he was a foolish young boy in the war who had been so stupid that he'd only been frightened ninety per cent of the time.

The weeks of 1998 unrolled. There were floods at New Year, winds in February threatening the roofs of barns, a shortage of hay after the year's bad harvest. His eyes scanned the pages for the name Rosa Calvo. It was a southern name. Not French, a gypsy name, Spanish or Portuguese, he couldn't tell which. Perhaps she came from far away, he told himself. Perhaps no one ever knew she was here.

And then he found it. A short paragraph about a gypsy woman reported missing. A man was arrested after getting into a fight in a café. He was an Italian. He told police he was in a temper because his girl had disappeared. Dulac remembered now that he had read the story. Items about jealous lovers, women leaving men, unrequited love, revenge, *crimes passionnel* or violence approaching a *crime passionnel*, all these had held a morbid personal interest for him. He had often daydreamed of going to the chemist's shop. He would have a pistol. There would be a scream. Then the loud report. Maybe several loud reports. He would miss several times. The sound of broken glass, the bottles on the shelves falling, would be pleasant.

Rosa Calvo, the unusual name he half-remembered like a character in a novel, was the Italian's girlfriend. The newspaper said how the girl, a Portuguese, had been doing seasonal work in the fields. Because of her 'itinerant way of life' it wasn't known if she was missing, or whether she had simply left the area. The lover was to have met her at Diderac.

She hadn't come to meet him. The story was of no significance. It simply showed to local people that some were not lucky, as they were lucky in Brittany, these unlucky others were forced to drift from their homes in Portugal, in Italy, in such poor countries, to live like nomads scratching a living where they could.

Dulac read and reread the paragraph. He felt excited, almost vindicated. He was not going mad, as he sometimes feared he was. There was some mystery here, and he had proved it to himself, if to no one else. He could see the expression on Baubel's face when he told him. Another woman had gone missing, another outsider disappeared, and her name was carved in the windowsill at Quimper's.

Dulac left the library and went to police headquarters. Baubel wasn't there. He was out investigating something – Dulac didn't pay attention to the young policeman who was talking to him. Baubel wouldn't be back till tomorrow, maybe the day after. 'Will it keep until then?' the young policeman asked. Dulac could see the smile, he knew the lad thought that an old man, half cut most of the time, wouldn't have any important business. Dulac left the station.

But he couldn't let it rest. He had to be sure. He was filled with new heart. He had something he must do. It was like the old days when he'd been young, waiting and waiting for something to happen, and then, finally, it did. What happened was love, and it put an end to him wanting anything to happen.

Dulac mounted his bicycle and rode slowly out of town.

18

The sun was bright even through the filthy windows in the kitchen. The warm light had something like an x-ray effect; it showed the shadow of the bones in her fingers. I do still exist, she told herself, the structure's still there. The whole world and Tom might have forgotten, but I know I'm still alive.

She hadn't heard Quimper come into the kitchen behind her. She jumped when he spoke.

'Come,' he said, 'walk outside in the air. You need fresh air.'

This seemed suddenly a terrifying prospect, to leave the kitchen. 'What's the point?' she said.

He dragged her to him by the chain and unlocked the padlock. 'Come,' he said. 'I don't want you dying on me, you must walk.'

'Where's Toto?' she asked.

'Gone,' he said.

He pushed her out of the kitchen door and into the bright sunlight. Her eyes started to water as though she was crying. Quimper led her round by the back of the barn and up a narrow path behind the farm.

She had trouble walking. It hurt to walk. The wind whipped her hair and took her breath away. Wonderful free-floating clouds flew across the sky, sailing over the hump-backed mountains, so free. It was too much to take in at once. She concentrated on the track ahead, step by step between the oddly shaped boulders scattered across the landscape. He let her stop to catch her breath beside a small waterfall dropping off an overhanging ledge into a dark pool shadowed by thick ferns. It was tragic scenery, she thought. There was a tall narrow rock that looked like a statue, a hooded stone figure, her rough-carved face full of suffering, looking down into the dark pool, her hands clasped, a tragic female figure covered in lichen.

Quimper shoved Anna from behind. 'Wait,' she gasped, 'please, wait a moment.' But he pushed her on. 'I can't,' she said, gasping for breath. She began to be afraid that he had brought her out here to kill her. She kept expecting a blow to the back of her head. He could hide her body here. In a year's time, if some tourist found it, they'd think it was the remains of a dead sheep and simply walk by.

And she was frightened by her own lack of fitness. Her lungs hurt; her legs were stabbed with pain; her head throbbed after the slight effort of that little climb. She expected her feebleness to enrage him, give him an excuse to beat her, but even so she couldn't move.

She dropped down beside the rim of the pool. She dipped her hand into the cold water and splashed her face. Quimper stood over her. She thought he must be sneering at her weakness, pleased even. She struggled to her feet. She wasn't going to let him gloat over her.

But his attention had been caught by something among the rocks. 'Quiet,' he said.

She could hear nothing. Her ears were filled by the sound of her own blood pumping. But Quimper was alert, listening.

A man suddenly appeared on the track behind them. He came round a bend screened by a single tree that clung to a crevice in the rocks. He was a tall man, wearing an old tweed coat. She recognized the fisherman.

She screamed, 'Watch out!'

A bird rose from the tree and flew away, calling an alarm.

She saw the man's face look up, startled by her cry, or the bird. But

126

he didn't see Quimper. When he did there was a look of horror on his face. He stopped, unsure what to do. Quimper raised his arm. He had a rock in his hand. He brought it down against the side of the man's skull.

The fisherman tottered. There was blood on the side of his head. He went down and lay motionless.

Anna couldn't move. She stared at Quimper in horror. 'You've killed him,' she said.

Quimper pushed her out of the way. He rolled the body into a crevice in the rock.

Then he took her arm and pushed her ahead of him back down the track. She didn't know what to do or say. She couldn't believe what had happened. He drove her back to the house in silence. When he locked the chain he said, 'It's just us now.'

He went out and she watched him come out of the barn with a shovel over his shoulder. He went back up the hill to bury the fisherman. She realized what he'd meant when he said "It's just us now". She'd seen him kill a man: he could never let her go now.

19

Carol lay in bed listening to the sound of traffic on the dual carriage-way. With a part of her mind she wondered why the noise always seemed so much louder late at night than it did in the daytime. It must be something to do with the uninhibited way people drove when there weren't many other cars on the road. The crawling vehicles in the daytime provided a kind of background hum, but at night even heavy lorries strutted their stuff with racing engines and screeching brakes.

But the traffic wasn't really what was keeping her miserably awake. The noise bothered her because it so exactly reflected the turmoil in her head. Her thoughts were screaming at her like an over-revved engine. Every time she allowed her thoughts to surge forward up the straight of a positive prospect she had to stamp on euphoria to bring them to a screeching halt.

I love him, she thought, from the moment I saw him I knew he was the only man I would ever want to spend the rest of my life with. There was no doubt about it. I'd never been more certain about anything, and I never will; we were made for each other.

But Tom loved Anna. He saw Carol as Anna's friend, committed as he was to finding her. Because he and Anna were as one, he saw Carol as his friend too, a made-to-measure relationship tailored by Anna. It couldn't be worse, Carol told herself. Even if Anna is dead, if she never comes back, Tom will always see me as he sees me now.

The worst thing, Carol thought, was that though Tom didn't know it, she suspected that his love for Anna was also an illusion. If Anna hadn't disappeared, Carol thought that she and Tom would probably have realized that they weren't really soul mates. Not soul mates like we are, she said to herself, if only he had the chance to see it. Now Anna's disappearance would preserve Tom's feelings for her for ever. They would never change, at least as far as they involved anyone concerned in his life now. If Tom loved again, it would be someone outside this drama, someone unconnected with Anna. I should get out of his life, Carol thought. If I'm to have any hope at all I should go away and come back when he's forgotten who I am. But I can't do that, she told herself, I can't leave him alone now, he needs me. At least I can make this better for him. And she said aloud, 'We've got to find out what happened to Anna.'

She gave up trying to sleep. The bedclothes felt clammy and her hair was damp with sweat. She got up and put on her dressing-gown, then lit a cigarette and stood staring out of the window as she smoked it.

Outside, it seemed to her that the world had drowned. Everything – the dark, blank-windowed houses opposite, the shiny pavement gleaming wet under the street lights, the black patch of unkempt garden between the house and the privet hedge screening the road – looked like reflections in water. There was not a breath of wind, nor a sign of a moon. It was like being surrounded by an underwater photograph. Carol pressed her hot forehead against the glass to give herself a sense of something real.

The telephone on the bedside table rang. It startled her so that she banged her head against the glass.

'Yes?' The pain made her sound aggressive. She never liked the telephone ringing late at night. The phone was part of her working life and in her own time it seemed like an invasion of her privacy. In the early hours like this, its summons seemed doom-laden.

She heard Tom's voice, cracked and rather faint. 'I'm sorry,' he said.

'What's happened?' she said. The blood was pounding in her head so that she could scarcely hear herself speak. 'Is it Anna?'

He didn't answer her at once and she almost shouted at him, 'Tom, what is it? Where are you?'

Then his voice sounded clearly in her ear. 'I'm in a telephone box,' he said, 'on a pay phone.'

Once she could make out what he was saying, her panic left her. 'My God,' she said, 'you frightened me. You sounded terrible. Where are you?'

She could hear Tom hesitate. Then he said, 'I couldn't sleep and I felt like driving, and I found myself near your place, and I wondered if you were up for a drink or something?'

'Tom, do you know what time it is? It's nearly three o'clock in the morning.'

'Yes,' he said, 'I realized that the second you answered the phone. I'm sorry. I couldn't sleep and I didn't think.'

'Nor could I,' she said. 'Come round. There's a bottle of wine here.'

'I'll be with you soon,' he said, but he didn't sound very happy, only rather desperate.

It seemed only moments later that he rang the bell. She had scarcely had time to open one of the bottles of red wine her flatmates had bought for a dinner party at the weekend.

She dropped the keys down to him from the sitting-room window, and went out on to the landing to meet him, carrying the bottle and two glasses. He looked gaunt, she thought, his eyes red with fatigue.

'I'm sorry,' he said. His voice sounded thunderous in the silence.

'Careful,' she said, 'you'll wake the house.'

'Sorry,' he said in a whisper which still seemed loud to her.

'Come in here,' she said leading him into her bedroom. 'No one can hear us in here. It's warmer, too. You got me out of bed and it's damned cold at this time of the morning.'

131

She got into bed and sat with the duvet pulled up to her neck watching him as she sipped the glass of wine.

'How are you, Tom?' she said. She couldn't bring herself to mention Anna. If there was any news, he'd tell her.

'Oh, I'm all right, you know,' he said. 'There's no news.'

'It's the waiting, isn't it?' she said. She didn't know what else she could say. Everything she thought of, the stupid clichés like no news was good news, sounded flippant and inadequate.

He looked at her and seemed actually to see her for the first time. 'I had no right to come,' he said. 'I'm so sorry. The nights are awful and I suddenly felt I really wanted to see you. Actually I felt I just had to see you, as though you were the only person who could help, and now I can't even think of a good reason for disturbing you like this.'

'I wasn't asleep,' she said. 'I was thinking of you. Perhaps it was some sort of thought transference. You look all in.' He was shivering. She realized that his hair and sweater were glistening with raindrops. 'Here,' she said, 'there's plenty of room if I move up. Get under the covers, for God's sake, and warm yourself up.'

He looked as if he were going to argue but then he didn't. That's how much he thinks of me as a friend of his and Anna's, she thought, he doesn't even think of me as another woman.

She watched his face as the colour gradually came back into it as he warmed up and the wine did its work.

'It gets lonely, doesn't it?' she said. 'I know how lonely.'

'Yes,' he said. He sounded bereft. He turned to look at her. She couldn't hide her feelings, all the longing she had for him was written on her face, all her sorrow plain in her eyes. He didn't know that, of course, he simply saw how unhappy she was. 'Poor Carol,' he said. 'I'm so sorry.'

He put his arms round her to comfort her. She pulled his head down to give him a grateful kiss. His hair was still wet. She could taste the rain on his closed eyelids. Suddenly her mouth was on his, his lips pressing

132

hers. His arms gripped her tighter. She moved his hand on to her breast and arched her body against him. 'Please, Tom, oh please,' she murmured.

When it was over he quivered as if he were ill and she was some sort of cure for what ailed him. She thought she'd best put the light out rather than have to watch him suffering for Anna again. But then he looked at her and there was an odd look of amazement in his eyes, as though he'd never seen her before. He put his arm round her and kissed her softly. She knew that he had suddenly remembered Anna. I don't care, she told herself as tears seeped under her closed eyelids. I made him forget her, he stopped thinking about her while he was doing it.

They fell asleep with the light still on. He woke her as a faint green-ish dawn light split the black sky beyond the uncurtained window. He was about to leave. She said, her voice muffled with sleep, 'You know, we're going to have to talk about this,' and he leaned down to kiss her forehead and said, 'Yes, I know.'

Carol did not hear him go. She woke when her alarm clock went off and it seemed as though she had dreamt the whole thing. Only the dregs of wine in the second glass on the bedroom table made her believe what had happened.

She was late for work but there was something about her that day. No one minded. She couldn't stop herself singing under her breath, even when she was actually working on a client. For some reason no one said anything or asked questions. All the clients smiled and tipped her more than usual. Everything seemed magical. If she wasn't dreaming, she told herself that she was enchanted. The last thing she wanted was to break the spell.

She took her break at midday in the upstairs staff room. It seemed to her that being a hairdresser was the best job in the world. Under her hands, careworn and dismal women flowered. She transformed lives. The women who walked out of the salon into the High Street believed, even if only for a few hours or days, that something wonderful might happen to them. Carol wasn't usually so conscious of the gift her clients expected from her, but when she was, she was glad she was who she was. She could have done something else if she'd wanted. Her teachers at school had been disappointed that she didn't want to go on to university. She had seven GCSEs and three 'A' levels, two of them, in French and Spanish, were As. She'd been mad keen then to be an air stewardess, until she found the job was like being a waitress only instead of a level floor, however hard, you had to push the trolley up a forty-five degree slope when the plane was climbing to cruising height and then dig your heels in to stop it running away when the plane started its slow descent. And after all there hadn't been many faraway places with strange-sounding names. She'd already seen most of them on television. What faraway places were left you wouldn't want to go to, at least not for a good time. And she liked working in the hairdresser's just because she knew what she was doing made no demands on her. She thought there was some sort of logic in that. She saw it as a recipe for contentment, being always in control.

She was alone in the rest-room. Thoughts of Tom banged at her head demanding to be let in. She didn't want to think, not about Tom, not about Anna, not about anything at all. If only we knew what had happened to Anna, that she was dead, or living with a millionaire in Acapulco, she thought, Tom and I could start again. I don't want Anna dead, she told herself, horrified at herself, I just want her happy with someone else while I'm happy with Tom. But that was fairly impossible when no one knew where Anna was. At least Tom knew now that the Anna he'd loved was not the person he thought she was. But might he think that the new Anna, the one he was discovering, was a more fascinating character than the old familiar version? Carol imagined Anna returning, reverted to her old bleached blonde eighteen-year-old self. In this horrible little scenario, Tom wasn't at all put off by the dark roots in Anna's bleached-blonde hair, or the cleavage and wiggling walk with a tight little skirt riding up her bum.

And where did last night fit in that scenario? Last night had nothing to do with Anna. She wasn't mentioned. Which was a first because before that whenever he and Carol were together he'd talked about her all the time. Which was fair enough. They'd only been seeing each other to keep Anna alive. Perhaps it had been only very nice and sentimental, a tribute to their loss of Anna. But it hadn't seemed like that to her. Not last night. They'd been two lovers without any ghosts, until he was leaving and she'd said, "We've got to talk about this", and she'd seen Anna there inside his head again.

Carol was so lost in her thoughts that she jumped when the door opened and Julie, the receptionist, came in.

'It's a casual,' she said, 'asked for you special. Mrs Turl.'

'Oh, God,' Carol said. The last person on earth she felt like dealing with was Sophie Turl.

But she went into the salon and there was the same old Sophie, with her hair like a blonde halo, waiting at the reception desk with the same old knowing look on her face.

'Well, Carol,' Mrs Turl said, 'you haven't changed a bit.' She sat in front of the mirror, touching up her lipstick.

For Carol all the magic had gone. She felt like an invisible junior. She was all thumbs, she tweaked Sophie Turl's ear with her styling comb, she dropped her scissors. It didn't help to notice that the blonde hair was thinning, dried out with too many harsh chemicals. Carol couldn't help feeling sorry for the older woman. She hadn't had an easy life, and she was Anna's mother, she must be worried about Anna. Carol felt guilty standing there at the back of the bleached-blonde head with all its split ends.

'I mentioned you to Anna's Tom,' Mrs Turl said. She smiled as she watched Carol's face in the mirror. 'He wanted to talk to someone who knew her, I think.' She smiled, then said in a voice full of pity, 'I was concerned at first that Anna was throwing herself away on a bank manager, although of course he's not a manager yet, is he?'

135

It seemed to Carol that her pitying tone was patronizing, almost contemptuous. Carol hated her. She saw the secret papery skin at the back of her neck looking defenceless and thought she'd like to give it a good chop.

'Yes,' she said, picking up her scissors. 'He came to see me.

'We haven't got very far in our search for Anna I'm afraid,' Carol added, and she thought she heard a cynical little grunt, but it could have been an involuntary gasp as the hair snagged.

Mrs Turl met Carol's eyes in the mirror. 'How was he taking the *dark secrets?*' she asked.

Carol struggled not to drop her gaze. She was hoping she had heard wrong. But she hadn't. It was hideous, Mrs Turl's smiling like that. The woman found the idea of her daughter's murky past amusing.

'Dark secrets?' Carol asked.

'You know what I mean.'

'Secrets?' Carol said. 'Everyone's got secrets.'

'Not you, Carol,' Mrs Turl said. 'Anyone could always read you like a book. I'll bet you did your best to keep Anna's dark secrets from the assistant bank manager, didn't you? But in the end I expect you decided there were just simply too many of them to keep hidden.' Her tone was sarcastic, she was enjoying herself.

Carol thought she mustn't let her get away with it.

'I didn't give Anna's photo to the papers,' she said.

'I don't suppose you had any they'd have wanted to print, did you, dear?'

The woman was a monster, there was no other word for it.

'Tom's very upset about Anna,' Carol said. 'He can't stop worrying about her.'

'I'm sure you're helping him come to terms with it, dear,' Mrs Turl said. Carol winced. She could feel herself blushing. In the mirror her eyes met Mrs Turl's again.

'I don't know why he's putting himself through all this to hide the

136

simple fact she's dumped him,' Mrs Turl said. 'I don't know why he can't just accept it. After all, he's got you to console him, dear.'

If she said 'dear' like that once more, Carol thought she'd stab her with the scissors. She put the styling scissors down and picked up the hair dryer, testing the heat against the inside of her wrist, then directed it at that stupid, insensitive head. She thought she should say something. She had to speak loudly to make herself heard above the noise of the dryer.

'Do you think she dumped him? Do you think that's what it's all about and Tom's made up the story of her disappearing to save his pride? That's crazy.'

Mrs Turl said nothing.

When Carol had finished Mrs Turl gave her a superior smile. 'Very nice, dear,' she said. 'It's useful having a little skill like hairdressing in case you find yourself having to make your own living. What I want to say is, I hope you and Tom will be very happy. Of course he's a bit dull, but if a girl like you can find a man to support her, he's worth hanging on to. You're much more his style, aren't you? I can't think what Anna ever thought she saw in him.'

This was too much, it really was. 'Oh,' Carol said, 'that's easy to explain; he's simply the only really nice person she ever met. It was the challenge of the unknown, don't you think?'

'Is he, dear? That's nice, isn't it? I must say, I wish I could have been so easily satisfied.' She got up to go, leaning forward to smooth her eyebrow with her little finger. 'I'll leave a little something for you at the desk, dear.'

What a bitch, Carol thought. But then she wondered, does she know something I don't? Carol was completely deflated, suddenly unsure of everything. Mrs Turl had managed to spoil it all.

20

Anna knew she would never come to terms with what happened in the hours and days after Quimper killed the stranger. She knew that she could never explain what she did and thought about what she saw Quimper do. It was too much for her to take in, too awful. It wasn't only what Quimper did; it was what she didn't do. She told herself there must have been something she could have done, but she did nothing. She didn't begin to understand herself. Deep down, she didn't want to face it. Something important had happened and she was reduced to a jibbering jelly. She knew that she should feel ashamed of this. She'd failed. She knew that; what she didn't know was exactly how or why.

She found it very hard to deal with. She'd seen Quimper kill a man. Worse still, she was certain that the man he'd killed had been trying to help her. She didn't know why she was so certain of that, why she couldn't believe he was a casual tourist or a fisherman who'd strayed into danger by chance. It would have been much easier if she could.

But she felt responsible. It was her fault that the poor man was dead. Of course she knew it wasn't her fault in the sense that she couldn't help being in need of rescue. She hadn't deliberately set out to become prisoner to a homicidal maniac. She told herself that, but all the same she couldn't convince herself that if she'd done something differently, if she'd done or said something else, she wouldn't have put herself into the position she was in. But what had happened had happened and a man was dead because he'd tried to help her. And whatever help he had tried to bring her had actually made things worse for her, not better.

Thinking that made her feel ashamed, but it was true. She was more afraid of Quimper now than she'd been before. She hadn't really believed that he would kill her or anyone else in cold blood. He did unspeakable things to her, he abused her, he could kill her gradually by taking away her will to live, but seeing him commit that monstrous physical act of killing a man terrified her. She knew that she couldn't judge him, or even think of him in human terms with hatred or anger or even pity. She found it hard to admit to pitying him, but it was true. Or, at least, it had been true. It wasn't any more. She couldn't see Quimper any more as from the same human species as herself and Tom, or her mother, or Nick Gold, or Carol Mouse. It made her more afraid, but it also forced her to see that she could not let him get away with what he had done. She had to face it, she might have to destroy him. No might about it, she thought, I've got to, it's a duty that poor dead man has laid on me.

She missed Tom then as she never had before. She'd have taken a year of slavery to Quimper for one hour talking to Tom. She tried to write a letter to him in her head, hoping it might help to sort herself out.

Dear Tom, the psycho has done something horrible. He killed a man. The way he did it, too, so casually, as if he was knocking a rabbit over the head. He picked up a stone and smashed the man's skull. He did it as though he thought nothing of it.

It was no good, she couldn't tell Tom like that. She tried again.

Dear Tom, I've tried to escape to you. I've prayed that he'd fall asleep and I could escape and come back to you.

I thought I could get round him to let me go, find some way to bargain my way out. I thought he was a crazy man who wanted a woman and couldn't get one, just a social misfit. He almost had me feeling sorry for him. I thought he was a victim, with many grievances from his past. How could he help but be a mad recluse? But it's not like that. He enjoys torturing me. I know he's going to kill me sooner or later. Don't forget me, Tom.

It was growing dark. She heard Quimper in the yard. She strained to create even the illusion of contact with Tom. If she could make him understand, perhaps she would be able to work out how she felt herself.

Dear Tom, the man Quimper killed, the horrible thing is that his death has brought me hope. Surely someone must miss him? People don't just disappear, his wife, his sons or daughters, his brothers or sisters, his friends will miss him and start a search. Then they'll find me. Dear Tom, I'll do anything to get back to you. If I can't get back to you, I'll try to find some way of telling you what's happened to me, that I was here, that he is turning me into a monster like himself. I'm going to kill him. Even if I never see you again, if I never escape, I have to kill him. That's the anything I'll do to come back to you, dead or alive. A bit of a poisoned chalice, isn't it, but it's all I can give you.

She felt tears in her eyes as she metaphorically wrote these moving last thoughts to Tom. She was imagining him reading the rumpled tearstained pages they'd find on her corpse. She could see the words on the tombstone, him putting flowers against the flinty grey stone – A flower plucked too soon to bloom.

She told herself, what twaddle! Instead of such sentimental fantasizing, I've got to think and plan. Dreaming up imaginary scenarios starring myself isn't going to help me. I've got to act, but both acting and action must be within the bounds of reality.

She had never imagined how hard it was not to give in to the temptation to escape altogether into fantasy. It struck her then why Rosa

Calvo had carved her name so carefully into the windowsill. Proof of identity. Then Anna wondered what they'd be saying about her now back in Godlingford, Tom and her friends, Nick Gold. Her name would come up, and they'd say, 'Such a waste, so young and full of life, with everything to live for, just snuffed out.' And that would be it. She'd be a token for them, a metaphor for wasted promise. And they'd be very careful themselves for a while, in case anything happened to them, as though she'd given out some kind of danger signal, a no-swimming flag where the tide of misguided emotion ripped.

She felt desperately sorry for herself, thinking of it. That was easy, too, another way of giving in. It took a real effort to tell herself, no, no, I won't let Quimper win without a fight, I will not die like that.

Quimper interrupted her imagined heroics by coming into the kitchen. He put his bag of tools on the table. He'd been drinking. She could smell it on his breath, most likely he was celebrating what he thought was his cleverness in defending his privacy against outside attack.

He was different. Perhaps he'd shocked himself by killing that passer-by, but she preferred to think he was feeling good because he'd enjoyed it. Killing someone would be the ultimate thrill for a freak like Quimper.

He actually poured her a glass of wine. He said in his thick accent, 'It'll do you good.'

The wine was still sour.

'Come on,' he said, 'like this.' He raised the bottle and took a long swig.

'I don't like it,' she said. But she wanted him to drink himself into a stupor, then he wouldn't do anything to her. She drank and tried to look grateful. There was no point in antagonizing him. He would start shouting. He was capable of screaming abuse at her for an hour or more. After that he'd start his horrible sexual practices. She raised her glass to him, encouraging him to drink on.

But he sat in silence, from time to time taking another swig from the bottle of filthy wine. After a while he said, 'I can't let you go now, you understand? If you try to escape, I'll have to . . . You saw me do it.' This seemed to make him sad. He leaned across the table towards her. 'What are you thinking?' he asked.

'Nothing,' she said. 'I'm not afraid of you.'

Go on, drink, she was willing him. Drink yourself senseless. Appease him, she told herself, stop him being angry. 'I'm glad you sent Toto away,' she said, 'I like it better when it's just you and me. He watches me.'

'Who, Toto? He watches you undress? The little bastard.'

The idea amused him.

'It's better, just the two of us,' she said again.

'Just the two of us,' he said.

He finished the bottle and got another one. He sat drinking silently. She watched him nodding but he caught himself before his head slumped down. 'Just the two of us,' he said again. Then he continued drinking until finally he crossed his arms on the table and laid his head down on them, muttering something she couldn't understand in a language she didn't recognize.

She was afraid he would pass out at the table and leave her chained all night. 'Please,' she said, leaning across and shaking his arm, 'will you take me to the bedroom?'

Quimper sat up, trying to focus. He was too drunk to see her. 'You want me to take you to bed?' he said. 'I'm too drunk for that.'

She got to her feet, holding on to the edge of the table. The wine had got to her, she wasn't steady on her feet and her head was spinning.

'Leave me alone,' he said. 'Another night, we'll have some fun.'

She put her foot up on the chair beside him to make it easier for him to unlock the chain.

He was so drunk he could scarcely move but he grabbed her leg and pinched her calf. 'You'll have to wait,' he said, as he unlocked the

143

shackle. He belched as his head dropped back on the table.

He had passed out. And her leg was free. There was nothing to stop her. She went to the door. He hadn't locked it. Outside it was black. There was no moon. She wondered if he had the keys of his pick-up truck on him. It would be too dangerous to start rummaging through his pockets. But in the moonless night she could run off and he wouldn't see her. She could reach the road before dawn. But which way was the nearest town? She didn't know.

Her head was spinning so much she had trouble standing. She was weaker than she'd realized. She had to hang on to the door or she'd have fallen. She felt like she did once when she'd come down with hepatitis after a trip to Turkey. She'd lain in bed for weeks with everything around her unfocused and nothing seemed real. She felt like that now. She told herself she could crush Quimper's skull, she could cut his throat with the kitchen knife or stab him with his own chisel. She could see herself doing all these things, but she did nothing.

She did not understand this, nor could she rationalize it. It was a fact: she did nothing.

Clouds drifted away from the moon and for a moment she could see the track leading away from the farm. Just walk outside and crawl along to the road, she told herself. But she couldn't. She didn't even work out that she would collapse within yards of the house, that she'd die of hypothermia before she could reach help. It all seemed to be happening beyond her, she could take no part in it.

She turned back into the kitchen and slumped on a chair at the table. I'll do it later, she told herself, I'll rest and when I'm stronger I'll get up and do it.

She fell asleep with her head on the table.

21

Tom did not return to work at the bank after his abortive attempt to save Mrs Turl from the anguish of believing that the body of a murdered girl might be her daughter. He was a little shocked that she should still be prepared to deal with the Press. He was sure her revelations about Anna's past had done everyone involved in the story a great deal of harm. But he knew how useless he felt himself, and he thought he understood that she would convince herself that taking action, any sort of action, was better than nothing.

He rang Duffy from a public call box.

'I won't be in today,' he said.

Duffy sounded anxious. 'Is everything all right?' he said. 'Are you all right?'

'They haven't arrested me yet, if that's what you mean,' Tom said. Then he thought that he was being unfair. 'It's all right,' he said, 'it isn't Anna.'

'I'm sorry, Tom,' Duffy said, then quickly realized what he'd said. 'I mean, I'm glad it wasn't Anna, but it must be awful for you.'

Tom was overwhelmed suddenly by pity for the murdered girl he had been unable to identify. 'It wasn't Anna' reduced a young woman who, a week ago, had been alive, living, loving, to an impersonal piece of debris. Tom felt more alone than he remembered ever feeling before.

He wasn't used to these feelings. Really he wasn't used to feeling much at all. He didn't like the way he was feeling. For God's sake, at the drop of a hat or a snatch of 'Men of Harlech' at Cardiff Arms Park he might start weeping. Not that he supported the Welsh Rugby team, it was the sound of all those massed rugby lovers united that got to him. He'd seen winning Olympic athletes on the podium with tears in their eyes at 'God Save The Queen', but the national anthem didn't have anything like such an impact at Twickenham. The English crowds didn't have the conviction of the Welsh. Or the Irish at Lansdowne Road. Perhaps, Tom thought, the English aren't great singers. He wasn't; he always felt embarrassed singing, even in a crowd.

He began to walk, not noticing where he was going. He wanted to shake off this new feeling of vulnerability. It's ridiculous, he told himself, Duffy had only said 'it' and 'was' and here he was seeing himself as one of thousands of millions of black holes trapped in their own tiny isolated solar systems.

Then he thought of Carol. He was not alone, there was Carol. He had never felt with Anna the kind of united feeling he had with Carol. But then, of course, he told himself, he had never felt the kind of disconnection he felt now from every other human being alive. And he hardly knew Carol. For all he knew, she'd given herself to him out of kindness, or worse, pity. Why did he feel so close to her, so *involved*?

He didn't want to think about that now. He knew that he had to deal with it soon. First he had to do the right thing by Mrs Turl. My future mother-in-law, he told himself. He hadn't thought of that before. How Mrs Turl would hate it. And so would Anna. She had totally eradicated her mother from their relationship. He wondered why. Did she love him so much that she didn't want to share him? No, Tom admitted to himself, that would not have occurred to Anna. More likely she didn't want the kind of life which included family ties.

Why am I thinking like this? Tom asked himself. He had never thought of Anna in such a way before, simply accepted what she told him without question. The person he'd known to be Anna had held no surprises for him. But that's because I never thought to ask her about anything much, he thought. He was sorry about that now, as though he had missed an opportunity.

It worried him that realizing this left him with a feeling of regret at chances missed. I should be determined to do better when she comes back, he told himself, but he had no sense of the future with Anna any more. Was this the beginning of accepting that he and Anna were over?

He had walked in a circle, though for all he had seen of the streets of the housing estate he might never have moved at all. He opened the gate in the mock-wood picket fence and walked up the path to the front door. 'Land of Hope and Glory' reverberated through the house.

Mrs Turl came to the door. She was wearing a dressing-gown. It was very expensive, probably an expensive present. She pulled it tightly around her when she saw it was a man at the door. But then she recognized Tom's bulk through the frosted glass. 'Oh, it's you,' she said, and let him in. He couldn't help noticing again how good her figure was. He wondered what she did for a living, that she could still not be dressed this late in the morning.

Mrs Turl smiled, seeing him look at her. She had a nice mouth. 'I'm on compassionate leave because of Anna,' she said.

'I came to tell you there isn't any news about Anna,' he said. 'I thought I ought to tell you something. The police found a young woman who'd been murdered. They asked me to identify her, but it wasn't Anna.'

'Poor you,' Mrs Turl said, 'it must've been horrible, seeing something like that.'

'I think they may ask you to see the body.'

Mrs Turl didn't look surprised. 'They are a pack of suspicious bastards, aren't they?' she said. 'But I suppose they've got to make it look as though they're working.' Tom was disconcerted that she appeared to take it for granted that the police thought he had murdered Anna.

Mrs Turl led the way to the kitchen and poured him a coffee. 'Do you want anything stronger?' she asked. 'I know I would after seeing a thing like that.' She leaned across the table and he could see down her cleavage. He tried to fix his eyes on the clock on the wall.

'Well,' he said, 'at least you don't think I've killed her.'

'I don't think anybody's killed her,' Mrs Turl said. 'I went to a medium. She told me. Don't laugh, she was wonderful. You wouldn't believe the things she told me. Oh, you think she was a weird crone in floating chiffon with a crystal ball. It wasn't like that. It's very scientific. She's famous for it. She's helped the police on murder cases. You should go. I found it a great help.'

Tom felt sorry for what he had been thinking of her. She must be out of her mind with worry.

'It didn't cost me a thing,' Mrs Turl said. 'The newspaper paid. Marla arranged it all. Marla, I told you about her, she's been writing about me and Anna. The medium said I'd definitely see Anna again. I said, "Not on some astral plane, is that what you mean?" "No", she said, "in the here and now in this dimension". I said, "That's the only dimension that counts with me". Marla wants to talk to you,' Mrs Turl added. 'You can't deny the publicity would help, keep the police on their toes. And the paper pays good money.'

Of course, Tom thought, she doesn't believe Anna is in any danger. His own mother thought that, too. Carol Moss had also thought Anna had gone off on her own, but Carol had changed her mind when they were in France, he was sure of that.

'Carol thinks something's happened to Anna,' he said. He was amazed that he said this. He hadn't planned to say any such thing.

Mrs Turl laughed. 'What are you trying to say?' she asked. 'And who's Carol?'

'Carol Moss,' Tom said. He knew Mrs Turl knew who Carol was. She was playing some game, but he said, 'You're the one who put me on to her. She's been helping me search for Anna.'

'Oh, the little hairdresser. Well, I'm glad she's been some help. Don't worry about Anna, she'll be all right. It's not just the medium. I know Anna. She's like me. You wouldn't believe the things I got up to when I was young, before I got lumbered with a kid. But it's different for her, she didn't have a brat to hold her back.'

She put her hand on his wrist. 'You go and get yourself a life, that's what Anna's doing.'

22

Something changed after the night when Quimper got drunk; the night when she had failed to escape; or to kill him.

He woke before her in the morning and he found her free. She hadn't run away when she had the chance. He seemed to think that changed her from his unwilling prisoner into a woman who'd chosen to stay with him. After that she and Quimper had a relationship. She asked herself, Why shouldn't he think that? That's how it looks.

And in a way it was true. She felt it, too. However much she told herself it wasn't true, she was afraid it was. It was as though by not trying to escape she'd resigned herself to being there.

She tried to tell herself that she was too weak, she'd never have had a chance of making it across that moor at night to reach the road. If she had made it to the road, the chances of anyone finding her before she died of exposure were small. She told herself she was biding her time, lulling Quimper into a sense of false security until she got a real chance. She hadn't given up hope, she was building up her strength so that when the time came she wouldn't fail again.

In her heart of hearts, though, she didn't believe it. She was only going through the motions of hope. She feared that Quimper was right, that she had begun to see her future bounded by those bleak moors and mountains and the tumbledown stone farmyard, living with Quimper.

It made imprisonment easier to bear. He took her out for exercise every day, like a dog. At first she could scarcely walk, but it was wonderful to breathe the harsh damp air and feel the clean wind against her face. He took her outside the confines of the farmyard onto the moor. The first time she saw wild rabbits there she burst into tears. They bolted for their burrows at the sound. It seemed to her impossibly sad.

So the days passed. The nights still brought his desperate striving for relief. She didn't care any more. She didn't fight him. She'd almost forgotten how it felt to make love with a real man, with Tom.

Except once. She dreamed about Tom. She dreamed they were together in a bedroom in a hotel – anyway, it wasn't in her house in Godlingford. Tom was asleep. She could hear his breathing. Suddenly she felt tremendously randy. She began to caress him. He turned towards her, fumbling a little as his wet mouth found her breast and began to lick the hot nipple. His hand was between her legs and she clutched it between her thighs, sucking his fingers inside herself. Her hand was on his huge erection, clutching the silky skin. It was so real she heard him groan and then her own orgasm made her cry out as they clung to one another and she thought that she would never stop coming.

Gradually she felt the soaked sheet cold against her stomach. She was confused, slowly aware of the room around her, and the feel of real skin against her, her arms entwined with a real man's body. And she didn't let go when she realized that the man was Quimper. She was still overpowered by the pleasure of a mouth that now gently sucked her throbbing nipple, the hand cupping her breast. She didn't care that they were Quimper's as long as the feeling didn't stop.

When it was over at last and Quimper got up in the early dawn to go out, she wept. They were tears of self disgust, of humiliation, but not only that: she also cried out of physical relief.

And after that she hated Quimper as she had never hated him before.

The weather was changing. The air was warm. Small bright flowers had sprung up among the boulders on the hillside. There were birds nesting in the eaves of the barn. She could see cows, bony from a winter in the byre, grazing in a pasture near the farm. The trees were covered with new miniature leaves.

'Come,' Quimper said to her, one bright morning. 'I've got fences to mend up the hill. 'The air will do you good.'

She went ahead of him up the narrow track into the hills behind the farm. He didn't trust her to follow him. This was where they'd been that dreadful day when Quimper had killed the stranger. Quimper's dog raced over and cocked its leg against a rock which could have been the one where the murdered man had been standing. She remembered how she'd scarcely been able to come this far that dreadful day. Now she walked quite easily up the steep path ahead of Quimper, although to be fair he was carrying his bag of heavy tools, a couple of fencing posts and a large roll of barbed wire.

They came out on a small grass plateau bounded on one side by overhanging rock. On the other, the fence Quimper had come to mend bordered a sheer drop. One of the old posts had been knocked over and the rusty wire was broken.

There were animal droppings on the grass. At first she thought rabbits lived here, then Quimper said that a sheep must have gone through the fence.

'Would it be able to survive?' she asked. She supposed he'd brought her to search for a wounded animal.

'Not a chance,' he said. He shrugged and made a hopeless gesture towards the broken fence.

She went as near to the edge as she dared and looked down.

She lay on her stomach on the edge of the quarry and looked over. The drop was sheer. A few scrubby trees clung precariously to outcrops of rock, their leaves like bunches of dead foliage on the granite walls of a fantastic palace in a deserted film set. As she edged herself forward to peer over the edge, she dislodged a few small stones. She watched them

153

cascade down the rock face and then disappear into the black satin surface of a pond perhaps fifty metres below.

Quimper was standing close behind her.

'Take care,' he said. 'That pond has no bottom. No one knows how deep it is. The stone for building the farm came from there hundreds of years ago.'

There was something about the way he talked about the farm and its history that made her suddenly full of hatred for him. She put it down to fear. It was as though he took it for granted that he and she were willingly embarking on a future together. It filled her with hatred for him that she herself had given him reason for thinking this and she was helpless to change it. And the loathsome quarry pit was a focus to her terror of everything that was to come.

She scrambled back from the edge. The place gave her the shivers.

Quimper was laying out his tools. He was kneeling on the short grass with his back to the quarry.

'Here,' he said, picking up one of the stripped chestnut fencing posts, 'hold this.' He held it out to her as he started to get to his feet.

She hadn't planned what she did then. She didn't even think. It came out of some kind of instinct.

She swung the fencing post like a baseball bat so that it hit him under the jaw. His head snapped back. He was thrown off balance and staggered backwards, clutching at air. She could see the look of amazement on his face.

Then she pushed him with the post, thrusting the pointed end under his rib cage to force him backwards.

He tried to clutch the post, but the stripped chestnut gave him no grip. He made no sound at all, simply disappeared over the edge into empty air. She heard a splash as he hit the water, then another, muffled, as the fencing post fell beside him.

She couldn't believe what had happened. She sat on the grass there, unable to move.

At first there was a profound silence. Then gradually a bird started to sing, and there was a buzzing as bees returned to a clump of buttercups.

Slowly she became aware of where she was. She told herself that Quimper must be dead. There was no way out of that bottomless pool. If he hadn't been unconscious when he landed in the water, he must've drowned by now. But she had to be sure. She knew beyond any doubt that if she didn't see for herself, she would never believe that he was really gone.

She crawled on her hands and knees to the edge of the quarry. There she hesitated. The earth felt reassuringly solid in contrast to the yawning emptiness a few inches in front of her fingers. She had to really force herself to lean forward and peer down.

The surface of the pond was all in shadow; the glossy water now looked dull and thick, like a sheet of muddied old plastic. Quimper's body, face down, looked like a couple of floating tyres.

She had seen enough. She jumped to her feet and fled down the track like someone pursued by demons. Several times she stumbled, but she leapt down that rocky path like a goat, jumping from rock to rock. Somewhere along the path Boris, Quimper's dog, came galloping from nowhere and ran beside her, barking as though it was a game.

She reached the farm and burst into the kitchen as though it was a refuge. She slammed the door shut behind her and shot the bolt. Boris, locked out, scrabbled to be let in. She was panting for breath, her heart pounding so hard that as she held on to the table to get her breath back, the heavy oak seemed to shake with its beating.

There was a half-empty bottle of wine open on the table. She swigged from it, the sour stuff so foul-tasting it made her choke. But it calmed her.

She didn't know how long she sat at Quimper's table. It was a long time. Then, at last, she felt her body jerk as though she'd been half-asleep. It seemed unbelievable that everything looked exactly as usual.

155

The ash was grey in the dead grate, the pans were set out on the range, Quimper's slippers waited at the door for him to return from the fields; her chain and shackle lay like a snake across the flagged floor.

What she did then was probably beyond understanding. In the early days after Quimper took her prisoner she'd imagined what it would be like to be free, even how she would feel if she killed him and escaped. She'd seen herself fleeing down the track to the road and stopping a car; or stealing his car keys and driving to safety in his truck. But when what she'd dreamed of happened, it wasn't like that at all.

It was getting dark. She stirred herself and went about the usual tasks. She lit the fire in the range. She filled a pan with water and set it to boil for Quimper to wash when he came in. She lighted the lamp because he hadn't come to start the generator. She made a meal of eggs and thick slices of bread, enough for him and her. All the time it was as though she was moving in a dream. And yet she didn't have to tell herself that Quimper would not come bursting through the door, stamping his feet and shouting at her to hurry with his hot water.

She wasn't even aware that she was thinking at all. Yet hours later, about the time when Quimper always unshackled her and took her upstairs, she found that she had come to a decision. She wasn't even conscious of what she had decided. She simply felt overwhelmed with a desire to sleep. Tomorrow she would come to terms with what she was going to do. What she really wanted was a few hours' breathing space, a few hours to sleep and think on her own with the doors open and free to wander round the kitchen without that clanking chain dragging on her ankle.

She slept where she sat, unwilling to leave the safety of the kitchen. When she awoke, a thin, pale light filled the room. The lamp still burned on the table, the flame flaring and the glass streaked with smoke stains.

For a moment she didn't know where she was. She panicked at the thought of what Quimper would do to her, and then she remembered that she had killed him.

She didn't realize that she'd already decided what she was going to do. She had to think. First she was ravenously hungry, and she went to the larder and found bread and the pale-yellow butter Quimper made himself. There were smoked hams hanging from the rafter, and a round waxy cheese on the marble slab.

She took the food to the table and ate as though she could never satisfy her appetite. She tasted blood, and where she bit, the bread was stained red. It was her gums bleeding, but the sight of blood brought back what she'd done. She had killed him. In cold blood. She thought, oh, I know no one in the world wouldn't call it self-defence. And justified. But I know that when it happened, as it happened, it was cold blood.

She tried to think rationally. She could set off to walk to the road and get to the police. She couldn't use Quimper's truck to get away. He always carried the keys with him; they were in his pocket now. Her mind refused to face the thought of the state of Quimper's bloated body in the cold black water.

She began to think then of what would happen. She thought of going to the police, explaining to them about Quimper, how she'd killed him to escape, what he'd done to her, telling them about the nights and what he made her do, showing them the metal funnel he'd used. No one would blame her, the man was a monster. And what about that poor stranger, and Rosa Calvo?

Then she thought, suppose they don't believe me? They might make out I wasn't a prisoner, that I went with him of my own free will, after all I was free when I killed him. What will Tom think? But of course he'll believe me, they'll all believe me: why should I lie?

But there would always be a doubt. There'd be speculation. There'd be endless questions. The police would want proof. Why should she think she could trust them? They didn't find her. They didn't get her out

157

of there. There'd be a court case. She'd have to tell the world he'd used a metal funnel on her like coring an apple. They could say she was promiscuous, that she led him on. She could be there for ages on remand if they accused her of murdering him. No, no, no, she thought, I can't, I won't. I'm going home. I want to go home. I just want to go home and get on with my life.

She began to pace about the kitchen. Automatically her footsteps repeated the familiar pattern of her movements when she'd been chained. It wasn't just the police, there'd be newspapers and photographers, questioning, elaborating, dredging things up. No, she told herself, I won't let them make me into some kind of a freak, a victim for the rest of my life. I won't.

In the end, she thought, all this agonizing is simply prevaricating. She had already decided. 'I want to go home,' she said aloud. 'Now, without any delay, back with Tom, back at work in Godlingford, back to normal. I want my life back.'

She got up and went to the sink, working the pump handle until cold clear well water began to flow, then splashing it over her face and neck.

Then she sat down to wait.

It might be days, she knew that. But sometime someone would find her. Quimper's cows, unmilked and unfed, would break out of their sparse paddock and stray in search of food. There was nothing for them on the moor. They would seek out other cows on neighbouring farms. The farmer would come to tell Quimper.

Then even a hermit like Quimper got mail. He was a farmer, there would be letters from the ministry, from feed merchants. The postman would notice and come to the house. Or he'd alert the police. And there was Boris. He had stopped scratching at the back door. He wasn't at his post in the yard. He would be scavenging for food. Someone might wonder what had happened and come to see. All she had to do was wait.

And when they came, her rescuers, they would find her there, shackled, helpless, Quimper's innocent victim. No questions, no doubts. No reason not to restore her to Godlingford, to her own life, to Tom.

She didn't move from the kitchen. She only stirred from the table to stoke the fire and get food and use the bucket she remembered to continue using as she had before when Quimper went out to work. Of course then he'd taken her to empty it every evening in the outside privy near the back door. She couldn't do that now. That was the worst thing, the smell of her own excrement.

She unbolted the outside door so it would be as Quimper left it. She even closed the unlocked shackle round her ankle so that the raw rubbed skin did not heal and arouse suspicion. It struck her that it would look suspicious that she wouldn't be starving when they found her. She put out food for herself as he had left it for her when he went out. No one knew how long he had been gone. It would have lasted her for several days.

She was ready. She repeated her story over and over in her head. Quimper had gone out and he didn't come back. That was the only lie she had to tell. All the rest, the car breaking down, the way he abducted her, was true. What she found hard was trying to erase the things she couldn't say from her memory. She had to know nothing, not about Rosa Calvo, nor the murdered stranger, nor Toto. She knew nothing. She was innocent.

She felt guilty, as though she was in collusion with Quimper in some horrible way. But if she told the truth, she'd never be free of it. Even if people understood why she did it, they'd always think of her as the girl who killed the man who kidnapped her. She'd be a killer. Women would talk about it, imagining what they'd have done, saying how they couldn't have killed anyone, or perhaps they could, but she'd be the one who had. She'd be marked for life.

23

The girl opened her eyes and saw Toto watching.

'There's someone there,' she said.

The man was on his feet before Toto had a chance to run. The girl was screaming. 'Kill the dirty bastard,' she shouted. The man caught Toto by the sleeve and knocked him to the ground. When Toto got up the man kept hitting him, swearing at him.

The girl screamed, 'Look out, he's got a knife.'

The man went down.

'You've killed him,' the girl said.

Toto saw her terrified face white as bone. Then she turned and fled.

He wondered if he should run after her. He didn't know what he should do. He heard the sound of the sea beating on the rocks in the cove. She'd gone. He forgot her.

He cleaned his knife in the sand. The blood glittered in the moonlight. He knew he had to go. He ran off down the beach and made his way to Joseph's house.

'Jesus Christ,' Joseph said, when Toto told him about stabbing the man, 'you've got to get out of here.'

'I was only watching,' Toto said.

'Look at the great loony,' Joseph's woman said, 'he's no idea what he's done.'

'We could put to sea,' Toto said.

'No,' Joseph said, 'there's gales forecast. We can't take the boat out.'

Toto had heard the angry sea, so he knew it was true about the storm. 'What'll we do?' he asked.

'You're not staying here,' Joseph's woman said. 'Call the cops,' she said to Joseph. 'The sooner he's locked up the safer we'll all be.'

'You can stay here the rest of the night,' Joseph said to Toto, 'but you must go in the morning.'

'Oh,' the woman said, being sarcastic, 'he'll get away in broad daylight tomorrow. Look at him.'

'She's right,' Joseph said, 'you'd best go now, while it's still dark. Go back to the farm, you'll be safe there.' He turned to the woman. 'Get him some food. He mustn't try to buy food on the way. He must keep out of sight.'

So Toto was on the run. The ground was stony and the walking hard. The soles of his boots were worn. He had a long way to go. But every now and then he stopped and fought the air, re-enacting the fight with the man who had been with the girl on the flat rocks by the sea.

He walked inland, not on the roads but finding his way across the moors and rocky hills. He was safe. All he had to do was keep out of sight. He mustn't take lifts, he mustn't shelter in the cowsheds of farms where people might see him, mustn't go into villages. All this was second nature to him anyway, he had always been like a feral cat.

Toto knew he should have killed the woman on the beach. It was the woman he feared. She would recognize him if she saw him again. Toto knew that people were repelled by him, that they didn't wish him well. Quimper had told him people were dangerous.

Toto was tired and hungry. He'd been walking since dawn and now, judging by the position of the glowing patch of cloud where the sun must be, it was well after midday. He'd eaten the food Joseph's woman had given him. He'd seen a village, but he hadn't gone in to find more to eat. He did what he was told. He was used to doing what he was told.

He was looking forward to coming home. Anna would be there to look after him. She'd smile at him. He'd tell her about the fight, but he wouldn't tell Quimper. If Quimper found out, he'd beat him. But Toto wasn't afraid of Anna. She'd tell him stories about Godlingford in England. He liked thinking of Godlingford.

Then he stopped thinking and began to hurry. At last the sheep track he'd been following emerged from the rocks and he knew where he was. He started to run.

As he reached the hill overlooking the farm he heard voices. There was something wrong. There were men talking. One of them laughed.

Toto stayed hidden on the hillside and worked his way among the boulders until he could look down into the farmyard.

There were police cars and a white van with green markings parked there. This was all wrong. He couldn't see Quimper anywhere.

Then he saw the legs of a man lying on the ground. The rest of the man was hidden under a blanket, lying still. Toto recognized the boots on the man's feet. They were Quimper's boots.

His first instinct was to run to him, but then he remembered what he'd been told. They'll hurt me, he thought. He stayed out of sight. He watched the men carry Quimper under the blanket to the van and then the doors bang shut. Toto didn't know what to do. It was a big thing. He had never known anything so big as seeing Quimper dead under a blanket.

A man came out of the house. He was a fat man in dark clothes. Toto knew him. He had come to the house before Quimper had told Toto he must go back to the coast and keep out of trouble. He'd been with the tall, old man who'd looked at Toto's hair as though Toto was a real woman with red hair.

That man wasn't there this time, only the other fat one. He was saying something to someone still inside the kitchen, but Toto couldn't hear what was being said. The man walked back to the kitchen door and held out his hand to someone inside.

Anna came out.

Toto watched her step out of the house into the yard. She stumbled and the fat man grabbed at her, holding her up. There was another man and a woman behind. Toto saw the man turn to the woman and point to Anna's ankle where the chain had been. The woman shook her head.

The fat man with Anna opened the back door of the nearest car and helped Anna inside, then he got in beside her. The other man and the woman got into the front. Toto watched as they drove away.

His mind was blank. He had no idea what had happened. There were still two police cars in the yard. He could hear faint sounds of banging and men shouting inside the house. He wondered what they could be looking for.

Toto started to shiver. Quimper was dead. Anna had been taken away. The light was fading and there was a sharp wind that cut through his damp coat, but he was used to the cold. It was Quimper dead under the blanket that made him shiver. He tried to think what he could do, where he could go now. He mustn't go down to the farm while the policemen were there. He wondered if Anna would come back. She'd want to come back for him. They could live together now that Quimper was dead, they'd be happy on the farm.

Toto watched as the shadows of approaching darkness fell across the cars in the yard and blurred the outline of the house. Then a light came on in the window overlooking the yard. The quivering beam fell on the box where the dog was usually chained, but Toto saw that the dog was not there.

He struggled to work out what had happened. Hungry and cold he waited on the hillside. Anna would be able to tell him what to do next, but they had taken her away. There was only one thing for him to do; he had to find her.

24

Inspector Baubel was on the telephone. Anna sat in front of his desk watching him saying nothing, simply holding the telephone and listening. When he put the receiver down she saw how his face and the bulky line of his shoulders seemed to have slipped a little.

She'd told him about the tall, old man who had come to find her and paid with his life. She hadn't intended to say anything, but she owed it to that old man that someone should know how brave he'd been. Maybe he had family who would give him a decent burial. He was probably religious. At that stage she thought all Frenchmen were Catholics and all Catholics were devout. It would make a difference that he was properly buried, she told herself.

She'd told Baubel that she saw Quimper attack the stranger in the yard and then drag his body away towards the hill. That way, she didn't raise more questions about her own story. She told the inspector she didn't know when she'd seen this, it was a long time ago and she'd lost track of days.

'It is as you said,' Baubel said. 'We have found Alain Dulac's body as you described.'

She shivered, remembering the sound of the impact as Quimper brought the rock down on the old fisherman's skull. 'Alain Dulac,' she said, 'so that was his name.' It was the name she'd read in the newspaper Quimper showed her. She remembered how she'd daydreamed about him rescuing her, imagining him as a young guide and sportsman, so different from the old man Quimper had killed.

'He was my friend,' Baubel said. His voice was bleak.

Outside, a truck had broken down on the bridge. There was a horse pulling a laden wagon; the horse whinnied and stamped. From where Anna was sitting, she could also see the red roofs of Goriac scrambling higgledy-piggledy up the hillside across the river. A breeze ruffled the papers on Baubel's desk.

'I'm sorry about your friend,' she said.

Baubel gave her a long, hard look. He made her feel uncomfortable. He was very formal, not friendly. She didn't know what she'd expected, but she'd thought there'd be some kind of fuss made of her. There'd be a fuss all right, she told herself, if the fat little French policeman knew that I killed Quimper. All hell would be let loose then.

'You say Quimper assaulted you repeatedly?' Baubel said. It was the first question he'd asked after he walked into the kitchen at Quimper's farm and found her chained there. She'd told him then some of the things Quimper had done to her. Plainly, the idea of the old man being incapable and yet repeatedly attempting to rape her bothered him. Now, in the police station, Baubel got up and looked out of the window. With his back turned to her, he asked, 'There was no misunderstanding?'

'Are you asking me if I consented to sex?' she screeched at him. She tried to stem the rising hysteria. She had told her story. Why did he go on asking questions?

Baubel shrugged. He doesn't believe me, she thought, he doesn't like me, so he doesn't trust me.

She was amazed. She'd never really thought about what would happen after she was rescued. She'd laid her plans so that there wasn't much scope for interrogation, and she imagined there'd be some gentle questioning, a lot of tea and sympathy, and then she'd be on her way back to Tom. She thought, I was the victim, for God's sake, this fat little cop should be feeling sorry for me and hating Quimper. Instead he seems to distrust me, and be keeping me here so that he can examine everything I say like someone unable to resist probing an aching tooth.

Looking at him, she realized that this was new ground for Baubel. He felt he had to use a style of questioning that was not his usual straightforward way with thieves or drunks. She could see he was finding it difficult to deal with her. Is that because I'm a foreigner? She asked herself. But I speak good French. It's not that. There's something in my manner he distrusts. He can't put his finger on it, but it's almost as though he suspects I rehearsed the answers to the obvious questions. Not that he can doubt I'm telling the truth. The garage mechanic has confirmed the electrics on my car failed. He found me chained with a locked padlock. He can't doubt me.

But nevertheless, she could tell he was wondering. And she knew why. He couldn't get rid of the impression that when he found her it was as though she'd expected him. She knew he couldn't prove it, but she'd realized at the time, when she'd seen his car bouncing over the rough road and hastily locked the padlock on the clamp around her ankle, that it was as though the atmosphere in the kitchen had been *stirred* by sudden activity. Her flurry of movement when she saw the car had created energy which she, too, had been aware of.

Now she said, 'I knew you'd come. I never gave up hope that I'd be rescued. When you walked in that door, it was the best moment of my life, but somehow it wasn't a surprise. I *expected* you.'

She smiled at him with what she hoped was the right mix of gratitude and admiration.

He sighed and was silent. She could tell that he was beginning to doubt his own reservations. She'd been found chained and the key to the shackle had been in Quimper's pocket when they finally dredged him out of the quarry pool. He'd got all his fencing gear with him. He'd obviously fallen as he prepared to put a replacement fencing post in place. There couldn't be any doubt of that.

He stared at her as though he couldn't see her. It was disconcerting. She found herself babbling to try to divert him.

'I think he'd done it before,' she said. 'I mean, I think he'd abducted someone else. He mentioned a woman called Rosa Calvo. She carved her name on the windowsill.'

Baubel had certainly heard Rosa Calvo's name before.

'Ah,' Baubel said, 'so that was it.'

She didn't know what he meant.

'We'll make inquiries,' he said. 'My friend Dulac mentioned her name. Perhaps he was a better detective than I. But Quimper is dead, we will have to leave justice to the good God.'

She knew that Baubel thought she should say something, show some sign of appreciation for Alain Dulac. He seemed to want to hurt her for her lack of feeling. 'Alain Dulac talked about your fiancé,' he said.

'Tom?' She was filled with longing to see Tom again.

'Dulac told me. He said your fiancé was here asking questions. Alain said he was with a woman, a beautiful young woman. Your sister, perhaps?' He gave a slight bow, implying that this was intended as a compliment.

She tried not to show that she was shocked and perturbed. Tom didn't know any beautiful young women. What was he doing with someone like that?

'He doesn't speak French,' she said coldly, 'I expect she was translating for him.'

But she knew it was obvious from the look on her face that his barb had hit home. 'He was a good man,' she added.

Baubel thought she meant Tom, but she was talking about Alain Dulac. 'I can't get him out of my mind,' she said. 'Did he have a family? I'd like to do something.'

'No, Dulac was alone,' he said. 'There was a woman years ago, but . . .' He shrugged. 'He didn't talk about her,' he said.

There was nothing more to be said. On the bridge, the traffic was moving again. She thought she would like to walk across it and stop and look down at the water.

'I'm glad,' she said.

'What?' Baubel didn't understand.

'I'm glad he was brave. It must be wonderful to have courage like his, not to be frightened, or to be frightened and ignore it.'

Baubel thought she must be thinking of herself, of how frightened she was as a prisoner of Quimper. She thought he wondered if she saw herself as a woman of courage.

'What about Toto?' she asked.

She had not intended to mention Toto, but he had asked her about him. She remembered that he must have seen him dressed as a woman when he came to the farm with Alain Dulac.

'Certainly,' Baubel said, 'we will arrest Toto anyway. He is wanted for killing a fisherman. We're looking for him.'

'Oh my God,' she said, 'I never thought of him as dangerous. He's like a child.'

'You can give him a good character when it comes to court,' Baubel said, but she didn't react to his sarcasm.

She got to her feet, feeling quite unsteady. 'I think I want to go and stand on that bridge and watch the water,' she said.

'You are free to do as you please, *mademoiselle*,' Baubel said, 'but there are reporters from the newspapers and television waiting for you down-stairs.'

Then she noticed that he was dressed up in a suit quite different from the wrinkled clothes he was wearing when he'd come into the kitchen of the farmhouse and found her. This was a big moment for him. He seemed to know what she was thinking.

'We must perform,' he said, and shrugged. She thought that he seemed pleased about it.

25

The newsreader on *News at Ten* turned to a new item. Thank God, Carol said to herself and got up and turned off the television set. She was careful not to look at Tom.

All evening they had sat in Carol's flat watching Anna on the screen, half buried in a tangle of arms and microphones. She hadn't looked herself, of course. Carol wasn't sure she'd have recognized the young woman she'd known as Anna Turl. This Anna was thin and drawn and mad-looking. She looked old, too, almost middle-aged.

Carol and Tom had watched every news bulletin. On the earlier news Anna spoke in French, which Carol could see made her seem even more of a stranger to Tom. Carol didn't blame Tom. Anna looked so thin and wild, like another person entirely, and she sounded crazy. Nothing she said sounded quite real to Carol. She talked about some man called Alain Dulac. Anna, who had been angry when she talked about the man who abducted her, was in tears when she spoke of Alain Dulac.

Tom couldn't understand what Anna was saying but he heard this man's name.

'What's this?' he said, 'that's the man I met. You remember him? The old man, the drunk, he was half cut. Did he abduct her? What's she saying?'

'He tried to save her,' Carol said.

'Did he?' Tom said. 'That's extraordinary.'

On the later news, at the airport in London, Anna spoke in English to the people from the BBC and ITN. The reporters wanted to know if the kidnapper had raped her and what sexual things he'd done to her. Anna didn't seem to hear their questions, she simply said over and over like a robot that she felt like she'd woken from a nightmare and she didn't want to talk about it, she only wanted to go home. Carol wondered what had really happened to her while she was a prisoner, and she saw Tom wondering, too. Then on *Newsnight* they showed the next day's front pages and a tabloid said Anna had been a 'Sex Slave'.

When he saw that, Tom said nothing. What could he say? He was numb. So was Carol. She didn't know what she could say to him.

She was sure, although they'd never actually said so, that each of them had thought Anna had probably run off with another man. She thought that as the weeks went by Tom had begun to come to terms with it. They both believed that if Anna had had an accident and lost her memory, her car would have turned up long ago. If she'd been murdered, surely her body would have been found. So she'd probably run off with someone else.

And here she was, something quite different and extraordinary, a victim of a crazy man. Carol's head was in a turmoil. What would Tom say? What would he make of it, with Anna looking so odd? And behaving like a mad woman so she didn't seem like Anna at all. Carol wanted to ask Tom what he thought of it, but she couldn't bring herself to question him. She dreaded the moment when she would meet his eyes and know that everything was over between them, that he still belonged to Anna. Nor did she want him to see what was in her eyes, because she was ashamed of what she felt. She loved him; she wanted to be with him, and she wished... no, not Anna dead, but Anna really gone out of Tom's life. Carol couldn't bear Tom to know that. She didn't want him to hate her, or to feel guilty about her. She wanted him to be happy. If

I've got to have a broken heart, she told herself, I don't want Tom to know.

So, ever since they'd heard Anna had been found, Carol had been treating Tom as if he were an invalid, at least some sort of a victim, too. Which, she supposed, he was.

'You should have been at the airport,' she said.

'I didn't know. She never called.'

'She called,' Carol said, 'but she'd've called you at your mother's and you were here. I'm sure she must have called.'

'It's just as well,'Tom said. 'I don't want our meeting in the newspapers. It's private.'

Oh, God, Carol thought, he's being a pig. He's feeling guilty and he can't deal with it. But all the same she was glad, because she saw a faint chance for her. He doesn't want to hurt me, she thought, he must care for me. He doesn't know what to do and nor do I.

Carol wasn't sure how she felt about Anna herself. It would have been so easy if it were a stranger she was watching, a strange young woman whose case she'd heard about in the newspapers but had never known. Then it would've been simple to empathize with the dreadful experience of a woman her own age; she could've tried to imagine how she'd feel, what it must've been like. But it wasn't like that, and she couldn't even pretend to herself or to Tom that it was. I should feel sorry for her, she told herself, I do feel sorry for her. I'd feel sorry for any woman who'd been through what she's been through. But there's something about her, the way she's behaving as though she'd *done* something, not had it done to her. It'd be easier if she seemed sorry for herself.

That's a terrible thing to think, Carol thought, I don't really think that. 'She's probably been going crazy trying to ring you,' she said to Tom, 'your mother probably told her you're out playing rugby; she doesn't know you're here.'

Carol let her head fall back against the sofa, closing her eyes in a gesture of weariness. She'd almost said, 'Your mother doesn't know about us,' but she stopped herself in time. There's no 'us' she thought, I mustn't put the pressure on him. She was trying to seem calm but she was afraid she would cry. 'You should have gone to her as soon as you heard the news,' she said.

'And if I did,' he said, 'what if they'd asked me what I thought of her being a sex slave?'

'Oh, for God's sake,' she said, being quite cross. They seemed to be talking to each other so formally.

But then he said what she'd been thinking all this time, he said, 'I thought she'd run off with someone. I always believed it. I never believed anything else; and the more I learned about her, the more I believed it.'

'Oh, Tom,' Carol said. She put up a hand to feel his face very carefully, like a child who's been told not to touch something precious. 'She'll be telephoning you,' she said. 'She'll be desperate when you aren't at home by now. She won't know what's happened.'

But she'll find out soon enough, Carol thought. She's bound to ring her mother at some point. Carol knew that Anna would never imagine Tom with her, but Mrs Turl would know. Carol didn't know how to say this, and Tom didn't say anything. Then she took a sideways glance at him and their eyes met. She flushed and started to say, 'Tom, I—' and he, too, was starting to speak and they both broke off, and neither one continued. Carol sat twisting her hands in her lap, those busy hands didn't seem to belong to her.

He took her hands in his. 'You're right,' he said, 'I'll be off.'

'She's going to need you,' Carol said. 'You'll have to be with her all the time now.'

Tom still sat on the sofa, but he was leaning forward, poised for flight.

'What's there to say?' he said. 'We'll have to wait and see.'

Carol sat staring at her hands, they were busy again in her lap, twisting back and forth, again they didn't seem to belong to her.

'Carol,' he said. He went to touch her hands but they pulled themselves away.

Carol couldn't believe what she said then. 'Didn't you love me?' she asked. 'You didn't, did you?' She recognized her own voice, but she hadn't spoken, she was sure she hadn't. Her fingers were twisting more than ever.

'Don't say that,' he said. 'It isn't true.'

'God,' she said, 'we deserve it, we're such horrible people. Mrs Turl won't keep her mouth shut. She'll tell Anna about us, just for the fun of it. Even if Anna dumps you, everyone in the world will hate us for hurting her. You heard that fat little French policeman with the moustache who found her – 'Such a courageous English girl' – as though she's actually done something positive rather than merely drive up the wrong road in the dark and meet a crazy man. She's the victim and we'll be seen as villains.'

Tom got up and moved towards the top of the stairs. Carol followed him. She didn't say anything, but he seemed to know that she was pleading soundlessly with him.

'Carol, please,' he said, turning to face her, 'there's nothing I can say now. I don't know what to do or how I feel. I don't know how I feel about Anna, or how she feels about me. I know I feel as though you and I were meant to be together, and I know you feel that too. But Carol, don't you see, it depends on Anna? This terrible thing has happened to her. I don't *know*. I don't know how Anna feels now, but she loved me. She trusted me. I can't let her down, can I?'

He gave Carol a swift, clumsy hug.

Carol clenched her hands and banged them against his shoulders. 'We matter too,' she said. 'Just because she's been through so much doesn't make her happiness more important than ours. Does it?'

Tom turned to run down the stairs. 'We're not going to be able to sort anything out tonight,' he said. 'When I've seen Anna . . .'

Carol said, 'I know, you'll be in touch.' She made an effort to smile.

175

'Look,' she said, 'whatever you do, don't say anything to Anna about us. Mrs Turl's a bitch, and Anna'll just think she's being bitchy. Don't tell Anna anything, not just yet. Whatever she feels, let her decide as if nothing had happened between us. At least then we'll know where we are.' He took a step down and then hesitated. Carol said, 'You can't let her down.'

'No,' he said, and he started down the stairs again.

The front door closed. Carol listened to the sound of his car driving off. She turned off the lights and went to her bedroom. There she thought tears would come and she could howl like a wild animal to express the pain. But she lay dry-eyed, her whole body filled with a dull, miserable ache she could find no way of relieving. Anna doesn't have to know, she thought, he doesn't ever have to tell her. Everything will be all right then. But Carol knew he would be bound to tell her; and part of her hoped he would and that Anna would go berserk and break with him for good. If he tells Anna now it's like hitting a cripple, she thought. After what's happened to her, I haven't got a chance. And a treacherous voice in her own head whispered, what's worse, Anna probably never really needed him, not like I do. But she needs him now, Carol said to herself, and burst into tears.

26

The telephone in Tom's mother's house rang and rang. Anna could see it in her mind's eye, the ivory instrument on the table in the hallway under the round gilded antique mirror that Tom's mother was so proud of you'd think that it had been in her family for the 200 years of its existence rather than being a lucky find one rainy afternoon in the Brighton Lanes. People were peculiar about their possessions and what gave them an identity. Tom's father's straw hat still hung on the peg inside the front door, but she was sure Mrs Pritchard had almost forgotten who the owner had been. She saw it as a sad little reminder, but neither Tom nor his mother saw it that way. Mr Pritchard had been dead for years and the hat was only remembered when Tom went out to do some gardening and put it on if it was sunny. She wouldn't have been able to stand such a reminder of the much loved paterfamilial head, at least, she supposed the head had been beloved. She'd have sent it to Oxfam, or thrown it away.

She let the telephone ring, thinking of Tom rushing down the stairs to answer it. After all, it was only seven in the morning. He was probably hardly up and dressed yet. And sure enough when he picked it up and said 'Anna?' He was breathless.

'You knew it would be me?' she asked. She wasn't quite sure how to talk to him any more. Last night she'd have known, but she hadn't been

177

able to get hold of him and in the end she'd had to call it a night, it had been so depressing being told by Mrs Pritchard that he wasn't there, that he was never there these days, that she supposed he was playing rugby, just as though the woman didn't know who she was, or if she did, she didn't know that anything untoward had happened to her.

So now she found herself, rather embarrassed, as though they were back at the beginning of their relationship and she wasn't sure if he would ask her for another date.

'Oh, Anna . . .' he said, 'how—?'

'I'm fine,' she said quickly because she knew he didn't have the words. But I'm not really fine, she thought, I looked for him everywhere at the airport. Apparently no one had told him I was found.

That had been a bitter moment. Two men had died, and she'd killed one of them so that she and Tom could be together again, and no one had told him.

Tom didn't seem to have any sense of the momentousness of the occasion either. He actually did sound embarrassed. Still, he'd never been good at expressing his feelings. She blamed his mother. It didn't mean he wasn't really moved, although he sounded so stilted.

'I saw you on the news,' he said. 'You sounded so . . .' She could tell he was straining for the words. It almost sounded as though he was frightened of her. She wanted to say, For God's sake, Tom, this is me, we're in love, we're going to be married.

'Oh, Tom,' she said. There was a silence on the other end. 'Tom. . . ?'

She hadn't realized how difficult it was going to be talking to him now. She was so full of feelings, she didn't know what to do with them. But nor did he. He couldn't help her out.

He said, 'Anna, are you all right? He didn't hurt you?'

He couldn't express how he felt any more than she could. And how could he, really? It would take somebody who was exceptionally in touch with his feelings all the time to say how he felt in these circumstances. Tom and his mother didn't have the sort of feelings they got in touch with very often. Anna tried to picture him, but all she could see was that straw hat in the hallway.

Why couldn't she admit that what Quimper did to her had left her feeling raw inside so walking was agony, in spite of the ministrations of the French police doctor? She wanted to tell Tom, but she couldn't. She said, 'I'm absolutely fine. I saw a French doctor who said I'll be good as new in no time. And at least I can give up weight-watching for a while,' he said. All I want is . . .' She hesitated, then she asked, 'Tom, there's nothing wrong, is there? I looked for you at the airport. I thought you'd come to meet me.'

'I wanted to, but—'

So he had known. She couldn't believe it. It was going to be harder than she'd thought. She could feel the euphoria of her dream of simply stepping back into their lives draining out of her. Where she'd been so certain, so happy in her certainty, she felt confused. She didn't know what to do. She'd wanted to be left alone. She'd thought that now and in future she could contain the damage that had been done within herself, deal with it herself. She'd been quite fierce with the do-gooders who'd rushed in trying to make her see psychiatrists and go to counselling. They'd said she must talk through what had happened if she was going to get over it. She didn't want to talk it through with anyone. What could they do? She could never tell anyone what had really happened. It was her experience, not theirs.

In the end they'd decided they couldn't help someone so determined not to let them try. They'd given her a list of telephone numbers and organizations in England in case she changed her mind. She'd flushed it down the lavatory in the aircraft on the flight back to London.

Anna felt flat and very tired. She had to say something to Tom.

'I know,' she said, 'you're right, our reunion shouldn't be a public spectacle. When can I see you?'

He should say right now, she thought, he should say he's rushing over right now to see me, but she let the thought alone. Tom was Tom. She'd never wanted him any other way. He wouldn't come rushing over because he should be on his way to work and if he didn't go to work, there'd be questions asked and he might, he just might, have to admit that he had a private life and that life contained her. It occurred to her suddenly that he might not actually ever have mentioned to anyone at his office that the woman who'd vanished into thin air weeks ago was his fiancée. That would be typical of Tom.

She felt horribly lonely then. While she'd been Quimper's prisoner, she'd talked to Tom in her head all the time. Their conversations had kept her sane. She'd told him everything. He knew everything that Quimper had done to her, and how she felt. She'd discussed everything with him.

But, she thought, of course I haven't, it wasn't *him*. It was all in my head. I created the image of the Tom I needed to get through it all, and I've come back thinking the image and the real man are the same. And that the real man understands what I revealed to my image of him.

But he wasn't; he hadn't. She'd never really been able to talk to him about her feelings, past or present. That had never struck her as even unusual as Tom was that kind of man. And anyway, she hadn't really wanted to spill out her heart to him. She wasn't that kind of woman. She thought, if I'd wanted that kind of talk, I'd have had girlfriends.

Nothing had changed there. She couldn't tell him what Quimper had done to her and she didn't want to. She'd simply have to bear it. She told herself, if I did tell him, he'd be angry for me, he'd take it on himself in some masculine way, and it would diminish the offence I'd suffered. I can't explain how, really, but I know that if I'm ever to come to terms with what happened, I've got to be clear what it meant to me. What Quimper did was a crime against me; it included my killing him, which I could never tell even Tom. As far as that went, Tom's protective fury and his violent reaction against Quimper was nothing to do with it. He'd be kind, that went without saying, but he wouldn't under-

180

stand. There'd be a distance put between us and he wouldn't be able to help writing me off as an equal person. What I mean is, he'd treat me as a victim, and victims aren't altogether equal people.

I can't have that, she thought, I won't tell him, I won't tell anyone.

She was still holding the telephone. She could hear him breathing. She needed time. She wasn't going to let him say he couldn't drop everything to come and see her.

'I can't see you now,' she said, 'the police . . .'

He started to say something, but she interrupted as though she wasn't alone.

'Tonight?' she said. And then she said in what she hoped was her normal voice, 'I love you, Tom', but he didn't say anything. She heard his mother's steel-tipped heels on the tiled floor of the hall.

She heard him speak away from the telephone. 'I'm on the phone, Mother.' His voice fell to an urgent whisper.

'Anna, it was weeks. I thought I'd lost you for ever, I had to go on . . . If I'd known . . .' He stopped, knowing he was making things worse. Then he said in his normal not-in-front-of-Mother voice, detached and cool, 'It's very short notice. I'll do my best.'

Anna laughed. When she put the phone down she started to cry, and once she started crying she didn't think she could ever stop.

After some time she realized that the telephone was ringing. It rang on and on. She knew it wasn't Tom. She thought she knew who it was. She was sure it was her mother, but she didn't want to talk to her yet.

The phone went on ringing. Sometimes it stopped for a moment, then started again. She knew that trick of her mother's. She hoped she'd take the receiver off the hook and then she'd know she was there and she'd come round in person. Anna wasn't ready for that. The ringing started again.

She cleaned herself up and went out. She was home, she was free. She wanted to wallow in ordinariness. She wanted to make the life she'd taken completely for granted seem real again.

She got off the bus in Godlingford High Street and the disappoint-ing phone call to Tom was forgotten. She felt like dancing. She imag-ined that this was how it felt seeing again after years of blindness – everything perfect, friendly, unexpectedly normal. She stood on the pavement among the people hurrying to work and it was so full of life: the buses, a young girl's hair glowing in the sun, bright flowers in a window box outside a café, even the stained grey concrete buildings that always looked as if they were wet with rain, buildings that were put there to make you think of grey skies when the sun was shining and the sky was blue, even those horrid buildings looked safe and peaceful. And everyone had somewhere to go, something to do, someone to see, there was much going on, no time being wasted.

In the queue for the next bus, people were watching a bank of TV screens in the window of a rental shop, all showing the same picture. A cheerful chatshow couple and two guests were gesturing soundlessly at the outside world through the thick plate glass. And then her own face appeared. They were repeating the pictures of her arriving back in England from the news the night before. The way she looked, so thin and frail, shocked her. She wouldn't have recognized herself. She didn't *feel* like the person she saw on the screen.

But whatever she felt she was inside, that haunted, gaunt woman on the screen was obviously how she appeared to the outside world.

'That's you!' a woman in the bus queue said. 'You're on the televi-sion.'

She felt many eyes on her. The whole bus queue was staring at her.

'What did you do to get yourself on television?' a woman asked. She sounded accusing.

'I was kidnapped,' she said.

The woman in the bus queue hesitated. Then she nodded. 'So you were,' she said. 'I knew I'd seen you somewhere.' It was as though Anna had passed some sort of initiation test.

The bus they were waiting for drew up. Those at the back of the queue gave her covert glances, as though they'd spotted something alien and dangerous.

A woman, very fat, the last to board the bus, said over her shoulder, 'My mother used to shut me in the broom cupboard, but I didn't get on the telly for it.'

Anna walked away. She hadn't intended to go to the office, but without even thinking, that's where she went.

Everything looked much the same as it had the day she left for the conference in Goriac. Only, all the posters featuring her as 'The Golden Girl' had gone. For a fleeting moment she thought Nick Gold must suddenly have acquired sensitivity, but then she realized that, of course the moment she became a crime victim she was bad for business. She laughed out loud. At least Nick Gold hadn't changed. Not that anyone would recognize that pathetic waif on the television screen in the glowing health freak she'd impersonated on the Golden Tours posters. Her replacement on the Golden Tours poster was a professional, she had that universal model's face which could have been advertising anything. Anna wondered what a girl like that did for an identity when it was all over and she was a fat housewife and had to figure out what it had all amounted to. Perhaps the money she made was enough, maybe she wouldn't let such things bother her.

Anna's arrival at the office caused a stir. They obviously hadn't expected her, and she had the feeling they'd rather she hadn't come; they'd have had a lot more fun gossiping amongst themselves for a few days, speculating about what really happened. Indeed, when she walked in, she was met by a faint sibilant hiss of whispering which stopped abruptly as she shut the door behind her.

'Anna?'

She didn't imagine the question mark. They weren't sure. Then they were embarrassed. They crowded round her and offered her coffee, biscuits, a chocolate, a glass of the filthy Asti Spumante Nick kept in his office for visitors.

183

She felt inadequate because she couldn't produce a baby, or a wedding ring, or a Caribbean tan.

Thank God then a flurry of clients came in and the crowd around her melted away. She went into the office where she'd worked, to escape. There was no one in yet.

She sat down at her desk. The chair felt different. The computer screen was further back on the desk than usual. She opened the top drawer of her desk. There were things there which weren't hers. Don't be silly, she told herself, of course someone must have been sitting at your place.

But it was a shock.

Nick Gold's secretary, Jill, came across the room to greet her. She'd always got on well with Jill. It was funny, she thought, that she'd never realized how sexy Jill was. She was holding something behind her back.

'Oh, Anna,' Jill said, 'it's so wonderful . . . We were afraid . . .'

She brought out a bunch of flowers. She was a little pink in the face, as though she'd been hurrying, and it struck Anna that Jill had rushed out and bought them when she'd seen her come into the office. They were fat, showy, greenhouse blooms, lush and lavish, brimming with synthetic energy. Anna stared at them and there were tears in her eyes. They were so different from the bright yellow celandines and the gorse blossom which had meant so much to her as they forced their way through the rocky soil of Brittany.

Jill misunderstood her tears and patted her shoulder. 'Great to have you back,' she said.

'I feel I ought to have been ill to deserve this treatment,' Anna told her.

'Ill?' she said. 'My God, it must've been much worse than ill. Should you have come in? We didn't think you would. We thought it would take months of counselling before you could face all this.'

Anna felt incredibly pale and feeble beside her. Jill brimmed like her bouquet with all the latest vitamin-added energy.

Nick Gold could see Anna now. 'Anna!' he said. 'Anna!' He still looked the same, only more alive, as if he were in Technicolor. The earring was still there, and he had another spot on his face – there had been one in a different place when she left – but otherwise he had the same healthy added-extra glow as Jill. Anna thought, I had that too, that's how I looked on the Golden Girl poster.

Nick hugged her. He smelled of some spicy oil. He must've had a massage before he came into work. She felt a little nauseated. He put his hands on her shoulders and held her away from him to look at her. If she'd wanted confirmation of how she'd changed, she only had to look at his face. This was a man who had always flirted mercilessly with her. She hadn't even noticed his insinuating talk and his roving hands; he was like that with all the girls. Sometimes among themselves, if he made them work through lunch or refused to pay for the coffee, they used to pretend they'd report him for sexual harassment. But now he looked at her as though she'd suddenly turned into a hag. He tried to hide it, but he couldn't. He was repelled by her.

'You poor little thing,' he said. He fussed round her, trying to cover his embarrassment. He manoeuvred her to a seat as if she had brittle bones. 'Are you sure you're all right?' he asked. 'If there's anything I can do? You've only to ask. Anything at all.'

Anna almost had to push him away, he was being so solicitous. 'Nick,' she said, 'I'm fine. There's nothing wrong with me.'

'Don't be brave,' he said. 'You look like hell. We've got to protect you from yourself. You must take a holiday.'

'Who's been using my desk?' she asked. She sounded like one of the three bears.

'Andrew's been sitting there.'

'Andrew? Who the fuck's Andrew?'

Nick looked relieved. She could see him thinking, that's better, that's more like the old Anna, taking no shit.

'Oh, for Christ's sake,' Nick said, 'you know, Andrew Symonds. He's been filling in. We didn't think you'd be back . . . for ages.'

'You thought I was dead; you thought I'd never come back.'

She smiled to show she understood, but she wasn't sure she did. It was rather a shock, to discover that life – her *life* – had gone on exactly the same without her. She didn't know why she hadn't expected it, but she hadn't. She was hurt.

She looked at Nick and he couldn't meet her eyes.

'He's not filling in for me, is he? He's replaced me.'

Nick was embarrassed, but she could see he didn't feel guilty, only sorry for her.

'Babe, what else could I do?' he asked.

Of course, he wasn't going to fire her, not yet, anyway. He wouldn't risk the bad publicity of sacking a victim of a horrific crime.

She wished she couldn't see his point. Then she could get angry with him. But she'd have been much the same if someone else was in her shoes. She tried to laugh off her hurt feelings. 'You could make a feature out of me,' she said. 'I could stand outside with a placard advertising Golden Tours, Holidays to Change Your Life for Ever.'

'Don't be like that, babe,' he said, shifting his feet as though he was itching to run away.

There was an awkward silence. Nick had been a good friend to her. She said, 'Listen, Nick, you're blowing up this one horrible incident into the only important fucking thing about me. If you do that to me, I'll never get over it.'

'Anna, calm down,' he said. 'I'll find work for you.'

The awful thing was, he *was* trying his best.

'What about Andrew?'

'I can't just piss on Andrew,' he said.

'Well, you're not going to piss on me.'

'Of course not. I'm going to take care of you.'

The patronizing bastard thinks he knows what's right for me, she thought.

She remembered Andrew. He was trendy, just like Nick. He was tall and fair, with a moustache, which Nick didn't have, but Andrew had an ear-ring, too. Andrew's image was good for the agency, it was the same image as Nick's. And Andrew Symonds hadn't been locked up by a maniac in Brittany, one of the UK's favourite tourist spots. Anna could see how damaging she was for the firm. She'd always been able to see Nick's mind working. He was saying to himself: 'Jesus, what a recommendation for a holiday, kidnapped, chained up, raped time and time again. What the hell does she expect?'

And what did she expect?

She wanted to get back to normal, back to the way everything was. That's what she'd thought. That's what had kept her going, was what she'd taken for granted. She wanted to go on as if nothing had happened.

But did she? She couldn't simply wipe out the experience and pretend it hadn't happened. She knew she had to face it at some point, but she thought that if everything else was back to normal, she could come to terms with it on her own, in her own way. She wanted to keep it private.

She looked round the office. Some of the girls were peering over the filing cabinet outside the office to see what was happening. She looked at Nick. It all seemed so second rate. Why make a song and dance out of it?

'I don't need it,' she said. She actually sounded kind, almost maternal.

She saw now that other people weren't going to let her take up her life again as though nothing had happened. To them, she was a victim and needed special treatment. Oh, of course, they'll try to be kind, she thought, but they'll treat me like a freak.

She went into the women's room to check her face and she thought, I *look* like a freak.

Two young women came in. They were talking about her.

'I mean, what do you *say* to someone after that?' one said. Then they saw her and they stopped talking. She saw the look of embarrassment and fear, mixed with a prurient curiosity, on their silly faces. They were wondering what Quimper did to her; they were stripping her naked and imagining what he did and what it was like for her. She felt sick. She went into the lavatory and she was sick. She could hear one of the girls say 'Oh' in a voice full of pity. And then, as they went out, she heard the other whisper, 'You don't think he made her pregnant, do you?'

It was no good telling herself she wouldn't allow herself to be a victim, she *was* one. It wasn't up to her. That's how people saw her, and nothing she could do or say was going to change it. She wondered what people would say if she went out and told them how she killed Quimper. What would they say then? Would Quimper be the victim then? And she'd be the villain, a killer.

She started to laugh. She couldn't help it. She laughed and laughed until the tears were running down her face and she was gasping for breath.

No one came into the women's room while she was there. She had it to herself. When she came out and walked through the office, everyone seemed to be working very hard.

She didn't remember going home. She felt very, very lonely, and yet she wanted to be by herself.

She was tired and she wanted to sleep. She went to bed without undressing, and pulled the duvet over her head.

When the phone rang, she thought it was Tom. It was her mother.

'When are you going to see me?' she asked. 'When are we going to have a heart to heart?'

Anna had nothing to say to her.

'Everything's up in the air,' she said.

'Of course it is, darling. That's why I want you to come home and let me look after you.'

'I'm fine, Mum. I really want to be on my own.'

'A girl in your position needs her mother looking after her,' her mother said. Anna could imagine nothing worse. Her mother added, 'You can tell your mother everything, and when you're up to it there's this reporter I know who wants to put your side of the story. She wants to do an article about me and you.'

'Screw that,' Anna said. 'Tell her to bugger off.'

'There's no need to be vulgar, darling,' she said. 'The reporter is a very nice woman. They're offering a lot of money. You'll need money now.'

Anna couldn't deal with this. She tried to think of something to say to get rid of her. She couldn't. Her silence obviously let her mother think she was considering the offer. Her mother said, 'You're not going to be "hot" for ever. You might as well make something out of what happened. You're an innocent victim and you deserve to get something out of it.'

She was incorrigible. Anna hated her. She couldn't stand the sound of her voice and couldn't bear the thought of being touched by her. She couldn't bear the way she wanted to exploit what had happened. But she was her mother. Anna was never going to be able to choke her off. Nothing she could do or say would get rid of her. She could hear her saying it, 'But, darling, I'm your mother . . .'

'Mum, I'm tired, I don't want to talk about this now. I'm waiting for Tom to call. He's coming round.'

'Are you sure?' her mother asked.

'Of course I'm sure.'

'You're sure about Tom?'

'Of course I'm sure. I love him more than ever since this business. It's made me appreciate how lucky I am.'

'That's not what I mean,' Mrs Turl said. 'It's not you, it's him. He must have told you he's been seeing Carol Moss. She and Tom . . . well, they're *madly* in love. She told me herself.'

Anna said to herself that her mother was making it up. She was jealous, she'd always been jealous. She'd say anything. But Carol Moss? Tom didn't even know Carol Moss.

Her mother said, 'Darling?'

Anna put the phone down. Then she took it off the hook. If she came round, she wouldn't answer the door.

27

Inspector Baubel drove to the coast. It was raining when he left Goriac and he knew that it would be raining even harder at the coast. He wasn't disappointed.

The fisherman with the stolen boat was helpful but Baubel could tell he was hiding something. They were in the kitchen of the fisherman's woman's house with the rain beating against the windows and Baubel thought he must press the man about the seriousness of the case.

'This is a murder investigation,' Baubel said.

'I told you he was a loony,' the woman standing next to the fisherman said. 'You should never have hired him.'

'He wasn't a bad kid,' the fisherman said.

'Not a bad kid, but he stole your boat,' the woman said. She was a large woman with a lot of dark hair like a gypsy.

'We don't know he stole the boat,' the fisherman said.

'Who else would take it?' the woman said. 'Let's hope he sinks it and drowns himself. We can collect the insurance and sell this dump and open a shop. A little shop somewhere inland, or in Normandy.'

'Ah, Normandy . . .' Baubel said, and for a moment he could hear and smell and taste his own country.

The man ignored the woman. 'Toto didn't know what he was doing,' he said to Baubel.

'As much as we'd like to be kind to a daft kid,' Baubel said, 'still, he's killed a man now.'

'We don't know nothing about it,' the woman said. 'We only knew he was a loony. Or, at least, I knew.'

'You didn't by any chance lend him your boat?' Baubel asked.

The woman laughed. 'He's soft,' she said, indicating Joseph, 'but he's not soft enough to give the loony the boat.'

'I didn't think so,' Baubel said. 'But did you see him?'

'OK,' Joseph said, 'we did see him. He was working here, wasn't he? He went out that night of the storm—'

'Crazy fucking loony,' the woman said, almost to herself.

'He went out,' Joseph repeated, 'and when he came back he was covered in blood.'

'You didn't think to call the police?' Baubel asked.

'He was always getting himself covered in blood,' the woman said. 'The things he ate, it'd make you sick to see him. We thought it was rabbit blood.'

Baubel saw the fisherman turn to the woman and make some sign to tell her to be quiet.

'He said he'd been in a fight,' Joseph said. 'He said he'd been watching and the man got angry and attacked him and so he took a knife to him.'

'Watching?' Baubel asked.

'A couple making love,' the woman said. 'He's a perverted bastard. When they catch him they ought to bring back the guillotine. What's the use of locking him up? It costs money to keep those perverts and then they let them out and they do it again.'

'I told him to clear out,' Joseph said. 'I didn't know the man would die.' He paused.

'It's all right,' Baubel said, 'I'm not going to charge you.'

'I'd have told him to run for it anyway,' Joseph said. 'He's not responsible.'

Baubel nodded. He didn't blame the fisherman.

'Would he be able to drive the boat?' Baubel asked.

'Drive it?' Joseph repeated. It was an odd way of putting it. He smiled and Baubel understood and smiled back. 'Oh, yes,' Joseph said, 'he was backward but he was good once you showed him how a thing worked.'

'Once you showed him a thousand and one times,' the woman said, 'and then only if he felt like doing it.'

'His trouble,' Joseph said, 'was that he didn't realize the danger involved. He was like a cat, a kitten, he had no sense of the danger of things.'

'So,' Baubel said, 'he might take your boat and just drive it off.'

'He could sail it,' Joseph said.

'Where would he go?' Baubel asked. 'Was there some place along the coast he had a special liking for?'

'I'll tell you where,' the woman said. 'He'd go to a place called Godlingford.'

Baubel looked up in surprise. This woman, who spoke with a strong Breton accent, had suddenly said the name of the English town with what Baubel considered a perfect English accent.

'Oh, yes,' Joseph said, smiling, 'he was always talking about Godlingford. It sounded like quite a place the way he spoke of it.'

'He said some English told him about it. It was all fairy-tales,' the woman said.

'That's right,' Joseph said. 'He said he knew an Englishwoman who told him about it.'

'Do you happen to know who that Englishwoman was?' Baubel asked.

'He made her up,' the woman said. 'There was no woman.'

'Do you think he was capable of making up such a place in England?' Baubel asked. 'That woman was Anna Turl.'

He could see the name meant nothing to them.

'Don't you ever read the papers?' he asked.

193

'We haven't got time for that shit,' the woman said, 'and the TV's broken. He can't fix it and he won't buy me a new one.'

'Toto never mentioned a woman being held in Quimper's house?' Baubel asked.

'He said he had a beautiful new friend,' the woman said. 'We thought it was just more make-believe. You couldn't believe a word he said.'

'Mademoiselle Turl comes from Godlingford,' Baubel said.

'That's incredible,' the woman said. 'The little shit knew all the time that the old bastard had her and he never said.'

'Could he sail your boat to England?' Baubel asked.

'It's possible,' Joseph said.

'Can he navigate?'

Joseph shrugged. 'He can read a compass,' he said. 'And then he would see land.'

'On a clear day like this?' Baubel said looking at the rain.

'Oh, yes,' Joseph said, not getting the policeman's irony.

'Would he be able to tell what land it was he was seeing?' Baubel asked.

'Do you mean could he tell it was England?' Joseph said. 'He could tell it wasn't France.'

'A patriot,' Baubel said, but they didn't get his sarcasm.

'He knows this coast,' Joseph said. 'He'd know it wasn't the coast of Brittany.'

Baubel left the fisherman's house. It would serve no purpose arresting them for aiding Toto. But the idea of the dim-wit sailing to England, that was disturbing. Toto had already killed once. Who knew what was going on in his head. He might blame Anna Turl for Quimper's death. He thought he should warn the police in Godlingford. They'll think I'm crazy, he said to himself, Godlingford isn't on the sea. He knew from the map of southern England that it was miles away from the coast, near London. The half-wit couldn't be expected to sail up the Thames and take an underground train or a bus to an obscure suburban town.

Baubel looked at the sea as he walked to his car. It looked rough to him, and he'd been told it had been like this for a week. He hoped the poor devil would go down in it. The last thing that English girl needed was a dangerous lunatic coming after her while she was licking her wounds thinking she was safe at last at home in England.

28

There was one moment, a few days after she came home, when Anna came close to wishing that she had never escaped from Quimper. Well, not really, but she woke up one morning and she thought she was back in the bedroom at the farmhouse and then she realized she wasn't and she felt something like sorry. She would have gone downstairs and spent the day in the quiet kitchen listening to the drip of water in the well and looking out at the farmyard and the bleak moor beyond. The gorse would be over now, but the heather would be in full flower.

It seemed so simple in comparison with all the complications at home. That was all it was, a desire to be away from complications she hadn't expected or asked for.

What seemed so simple, in her half-awake state, was communicating with the Tom she'd talked to by the hour in her head in Quimper's kitchen, compared to trying to communicate with Tom now. And as she sat up in bed and turned off the alarm clock, she found herself thinking that perhaps that imaginary Tom was the man she was in love with, not with the real person at all.

The two of them had spent hours every day pretending that everything was normal, but neither of them seemed to be able to say the right thing. She cried a lot, and he tried not to lose his temper and instead he sulked because he couldn't find words to say what he felt.

He wasn't the only one. Everyone she knew from what she'd begun to call the Old Days BQ, meaning Before Quimper, had problems knowing what to say to her. And she didn't seem to be able to open her mouth without embarrassing them. This seemed to apply to anyone, from the postman and the girl behind the counter at the newsagents to the garage man and the doctor. She didn't even include her mother, because they had never been able to talk to any purpose. That hadn't changed. Every time Mrs Turl rang or called round she said something which got on Anna's nerves and Anna would shout at her and then they'd be at it like cat and dog, all the resentment and bitterness between them boiling over until Mrs Turl stormed out or Anna put the phone down. At least that was genuine communication of a kind, but for Anna it was irrelevant and pointless. It had nothing to do with what had happened to her in Brittany. Quarrelling with her mother about the past drained her of energy she needed to sort out her life in the present.

She didn't blame anyone for being as they were. It wasn't their fault. There just simply wasn't an accepted form of behaviour to cover being natural with someone who's been abducted, raped and imprisoned by a maniac, let alone someone who had to kill her jailor to escape. Anna knew how people felt. She'd crossed streets to avoid meeting a girlfriend who'd lost her toddler in a car accident because she didn't know what to say. It wasn't that she wasn't desperately sorry and wanted to offer help, but she knew she had nothing to offer that would help. Anna could understand that people didn't know what to say in support, and because she knew that, and that they were right, they couldn't help, she was embarrassed as well as embarrassing.

But she and Tom had to work through the barriers if they were going to reclaim their relationship. They were not getting anywhere.

The night before Anna woke up almost nostalgic for Quimper's kitchen, she and Tom had made love for the first time since she returned.

It started off fine, gloriously familiar. It was wonderful, she thought, discovering his body once again. She made no effort to hide how much she wanted him. She craved him. She was beside herself, gripping him as if she would never let him go.

But he was gentle, sweet, treating her like precious porcelain. She wanted him to be forceful, to dominate, to meet the violence of her passion with violence of his own. And when he didn't, she was suddenly furious. She wanted to hurt him.

He couldn't do it. He lost his erection and slipped softly out of her.

'I'm so sorry' he whispered. 'I'm so sorry. I can't.'

For some time they lay there together. Anna had never felt so alone. There was no way she could find to bridge the gulf that had opened between them.

Much later, she asked him, 'Is it because of Quimper? What he did to me?'

She felt him shake his head. He didn't speak.

'The other things, then? The things you read about me in the news-papers?'

'No,' he said, so softly she could scarcely hear.

She was overwhelmed by a wave of loathing for her mother. Sophie Turl had shown her the newspaper cuttings she'd cut out about her daughter as though she was proud that she had made Anna famous.

'It's not that,' Tom said. 'I don't know why.'

'Tom, tell me honestly, don't you love me any more?'

'This kind of thing happens to everyone,' he said.

'Tell me,' she said.

'I don't know,' he said. 'I don't know what I feel.'

'No,' she said, 'nor do I. Perhaps that's a start.'

29

In Godlingford's municipal park two women, one a young mother with a baby in a pushchair, the other an older woman leading a toddler by the hand, stopped to watch the curious antics of the young tramp at the water's edge.

'What's he doing?' the young mother asked.

The older woman pulled the toddler close to her knee. 'God knows,' she said, in the hushed, respectful voice of one speaking within earshot of a madman. 'He must be one of those mental patients they've let loose on the community.'

'He's so young,' the young mother said. 'It's a scandal. He could be dangerous.'

They stood and watched as Toto, crouching low, crept towards the edge of the ornamental lake.

'What's he got in his hand?' the older woman asked. 'Is it a crucifix?' Lunatics, she knew, often had a religious obsession.

'It's a catapult,' the young mother said, and then there was alarm in her voice. 'Oh, my God, he's trying to kill one of the ducks.'

The older woman snatched up the toddler. 'Quick,' she said, turning to run, 'call the police.' The young mother grabbed the baby and hurried after her, leaving the pushchair tipped sideways on the grass.

Toto swore under his breath as the birds at the edge of the lake scattered with loud cries of alarm. He was hungry. How did people live in a place like this? There was no point in waiting for the birds to return now. They wouldn't come back, not for some time. He made for a bank of rhododendron bushes where he'd spent the night.

Toto was used to sleeping out. It seemed natural to him. But food preoccupied him. It had always been easy enough to come by before, no lack of small animals to snare, every farm had vegetables, and there were always fish on the coast. But here it was different. They didn't have proper gardens, just little patches of flowers and hedges. He'd tried to buy food with his French money but the shopkeeper wouldn't take it. Most of all it was people who got in his way. There were people everywhere, all in each other's way, like those two women screeching when he tried to shoot a duck with his catapult. And earlier, a man had shouted and come at him with a stick. But Toto was patient. He didn't think in terms of difficulty, he simply tried something else. He'd come to find Anna, and though he had no idea how to go about this, he wouldn't give up. He didn't wonder how. He saw nothing in any other context except the object of his immediate intention.

Crossing the Channel had been easy enough, though in any case it hadn't occurred to him to think it would be difficult. He'd watched Joseph leave the boat to go to the bar on the quay. He saw Joseph lock the hatch and tuck the key under the engine cover. Then he simply went aboard and stole the boat.

Several hours later, he ran her aground on a long deserted stretch of sand dune and reed close to a refinery chimney belching yellowish smoke.

He took no notice of his wet jeans and soaked shoes as he walked away from the sea across a grim, dirty landscape of scrubby flatlands and huge warehouse-like buildings, looking for the docks. He made his way to a lorry park, making to anyone he met the hitch-hiker's gesture with his thumb and the word 'Godlingford'.

The men laughed when they spoke to him. He didn't understand.

They gathered round him, trying to make out what he wanted. Then a big fellow pushed Toto towards a lorry. 'Oh, what the hell,' he said to the others, 'I've a delivery in Croydon. I'll drop him on the way. Get in,' he said to Toto. '*Allez, allez*, Pierre.' The other men laughed. The big truck driver turned and smiled.

They travelled through what seemed to Toto an endless built-up area. The whole time he sat up straight watching the road ahead, waiting for the moment he would sight Godlingford, the happy place of Anna's stories. But there was nothing special about the stretch of road where the driver drew into the side and stopped the lorry, announcing, 'That's it, mate. This is Godlingford.' Toto thought it was a trick. The driver leaned across and opened Toto's door. 'Out,' he said, pushing him. Then he shouted, '*Au revoir*,' and pulled the door shut. Then he drove off.

Toto saw the town but he didn't know what to do. He walked until he saw trees and bushes and he hid in them. He spent the night there.

In the morning he walked away from the park. The traffic on one side of the road was moving slowly, crawling three abreast, a long queue of cars, and the biggest buses he had ever seen. On the other side of the road, the traffic was light, moving freely. He followed the slow-moving stream where most people were going.

He stood among the crowd of hurrying people. The taste of the air was foul. People knocked into him. They were irritated, sometimes they snapped at him. He asked several times 'Godlingford?' from passers-by, but they took no notice. This was not the place of Anna's fairy-tales. He wandered on.

And then he saw something he recognized. There was the Château de Goriac in a shop window. The great grey turrets of the château rose to a familiar sky, a smiling couple stood in the picture, wearing beautiful clothes, the woman leaning against a shiny red car outside the Chateau entrance, the man, an obvious visitor, was smoking a pipe.

People went in and out of the shop with the picture of the Château de Goriac in the window. He saw shadowy figures moving inside through the thick plate glass. Toto backed away. The men might be dangerous. And then he saw Anna. She came out of the shop between two men. One was small and skinny like a weasel, the kind of man Toto expected to carry a knife. The other was tall and had a moustache. Both the men had ear-rings.

Toto moved back out of sight, then followed behind them as they walked up the street. Toto could tell Anna knew them well. The tall man with the moustache stopped at a street corner and made a gesture of farewell.

'Goodnight, Andrew,' Toto heard the other man call, but he did not know what it meant.

Anna and the small man stopped outside a tall, grey concrete block. Anna and the man talked, both of them gesticulating. Anna kept saying, 'No, no.' Toto knew that word. He felt for his own knife and looked at the man carefully, trying to see where he might be hiding his, but his clothes hung too loosely to show.

There was a stream of cars coming out of the building. The man tried to take Anna away but she resisted him. Then the man shrugged his shoulders and went into the building, shouting something back at her over his shoulder. Anna walked away.

Toto followed. He was certain she didn't like either of the men, but he didn't think Anna was afraid of them. She was free. She wasn't being held against her will. Toto's head hurt as he tried to sort out his thoughts.

He followed her until she joined a queue outside a shop. Anna was impatient. She moved from one foot to the other, constantly stepping into the road to peer ahead through the oncoming traffic. At last she pushed her way out of the queue and began to walk. He followed her easily even with the crowds on the pavement, but then there were no more shops, only houses and no more crowd for him to hide in. He had to be careful in case she looked round and saw him. She turned down a narrow paved alley between high walls. This took her out into a broad stretch of grass bounded on three sides by rows of small, brightly coloured terraced cottages.

Suddenly she broke into a run. This took Toto by surprise. He didn't run after her. He didn't want to be noticed. He walked faster, but warily, keeping an eye on the cars parked at the kerb, they would offer cover if she turned round.

But she didn't turn. She hurried to open the front door of one of the cottages. It was a blue door with panels of coloured glass. A light went on in the ground-floor window. Toto watched as Anna moved across the room. He could see through the room into a small garden at the back of the house. The light in that room went off and a little later the upstairs window lighted up. Toto settled down to wait. He recognized this place with the pretty blue door. This was the house she meant when she told him the stories. This was Godlingford.

30

Anna wanted something positive to happen. She wanted action, to take action. That was the only way she could see to break away from the kind of inertia she'd been going through, simply waiting for things to happen. And nothing had happened. She had to *do* something.

It had been a mistake to go back to the office to see Nick, though. She'd thought she was ready to go back to work, and, frankly, she could do with the money. Nick wasn't ready, though. He offered her money; he wanted to pay her sick leave. She knew he was paying her to stay away. He had walked with her out of the office and offered to drive her home. The thought that he might feel he had to offer her a charitable fuck made her feel sick.

When she got home she looked up Carol Moss's number in the telephone directory to find her address. Anna couldn't forget the way her mother had mentioned Tom and Carol Moss together, as though there was something between them. She hadn't believed her then, and she didn't really now, but she wanted to hear Carol tell her it wasn't true. And if it was, she wanted Carol to tell her that it was.

She called a taxi. She didn't call Carol, there was no point giving her a chance to concoct a story, if there was a story.

She noticed a young man, or a girl, she wasn't sure which, waiting at the corner of the alley that ran behind the terrace of cottages. There was a glimpse of red hair. It gave her quite a turn; it looked like Toto. She told herself paranoia was part of her new victimhood. She wondered what Toto was doing. They'd probably put him in an institution. Poor Toto, it wasn't his fault. It all seemed very far away.

The taxi driver wanted to talk. 'What do you think of our local excitement?'

'What excitement was that?'

'That girl that went missing a few weeks back, she was found chained up by a sex fiend in a château.'

'Is that right?' Anna said. She could see the driver thought she should be taking more interest.

'Mind you,' he said, 'maybe she wasn't everything she should've been, know what I mean? There was a lot of stuff come out about her. She was a right little raver. But no one deserves what happened to her, getting herself snatched by one of those sexual perverts. They ought to string up the lot of them.'

'We must be getting close,' she said.

The taxi driver slowed, then stopped. He looked Anna up and down as she leaned across to pay him. 'Hey, it's you, isn't it?'

'That's right,' she said. It was less trouble to agree than to argue with him.

She'd offended him, not saying who she was earlier. He'd missed an opportunity to get prurient answers from the horse's mouth. She watched as he swung angrily across the central reservation in an illegal U-turn. It seemed to her that in spite of herself, something odd had happened. She'd become public property. She belonged to everyone now, their own famous victim. That man really thought she had no right to hide her identity like that. Like what? she thought. She hadn't pretended not to be herself. He'd been slow to recognize her, but he'd blamed her for not telling him at once. He'd assumed she owed him that in return for his compassion.

There were lights on in Carol's house. When Anna rang the bell she heard her galloping down the stairs. Carol opened the door in a rush, her face eager. She was obviously expecting someone and it wasn't Anna. She looked disappointed when she saw who her visitor was, but Anna caught something in her expression, something between fear and guilt, which made her suddenly certain that her mother was right. Carol had expected her to be Tom.

Carol went white when she saw Anna. 'What's happened?' she asked. 'Is it Tom?'

'No,' Anna said. She was taken aback by her concern. She didn't know why, but she hadn't expected Carol to *care* so much. Otherwise Carol dealt with the shock of seeing Anna pretty well, asking her in and making the right conventional noises about how long it had been since they'd seen each other, and how awful it must've been being taken prisoner by a maniac.

By the time they'd gone through it all, Anna was sitting in the room upstairs and Carol had opened a bottle of red wine and poured them both glasses.

Without make-up and with her head wrapped in a towel, Carol still looked almost the same as she'd done in the sixth form at school. She'd suffered from acne then, it was gone but she hadn't lost her puppy fat. She still looked overweight, or what Anna's mother used to describe as 'cuddly'.

Briefly, Anna felt relieved. At first glance she thought Carol didn't seem to offer a lot of competition. And then she caught sight of herself reflected in the glass of a picture on the opposite wall and she was reminded what she really looked like. What Carol had was warmth and vitality and generosity in abundance, and Anna could see exactly what Tom, or any other man, would see in her. She had a momentary vision of the two of them growing old together, like two comfortable slippers beside the fire. She had never seen herself and Tom that way.

'So it's true.' Anna said. She didn't realize she'd spoken aloud.

'What's true?'

209

'You were the one in France, the woman with Tom.'

Anna wondered why she was there, what she'd thought she could gain by confronting Carol.

'We went to France to look for you,' Carol said, and then she added, 'We couldn't find any trace of you.'

'My mother told me you and Tom are together.'

As Anna said this she could hear how unconvincing it sounded. Carol was the one person in the world who knew as well as she did herself what a manipulative liar Mrs Turl was. Her word was such flimsy evidence that Anna felt she had to apologize. 'I'm sorry,' she said, 'it's just that when she said it . . . I don't know what came over me, it must be something to do with what's happened to me . . .'

But she could see Carol was thinking, I've brought this on myself, and now I've got to go through with it. Carol had never been able to hide her feelings.

'Anna, we need to talk,' Carol said.

Anna looked at her and Carol turned into a stranger before her eyes. It seemed incredible that this was someone she was once close to. She was like a different person, whom she didn't recognize. And she seemed just as ill-at-ease with Anna, as though Anna had got a contagious disease.

'I'm sorry, Anna, but I couldn't help it. I love him,' Carol said. 'And I think he loves me back. We could be happy together. It's a fact. We didn't want it to happen, but it did.'

Anna looked around, trying to gather her wits together. Whatever Tom felt about it, this thing was obviously serious for Carol. She loved him. She didn't try to hide it. Anna could see Tom wasn't living there, not with two other girls sharing the bathroom. One of the flatmates obviously smoked. There was a dirty ashtray on the coffee table. Tom wouldn't even want to stay over with someone who smoked in the house.

Carol sat on the sofa with her legs tucked under her. She was trying

210

A TURN IN THE ROAD

to look at ease, but her hands were shaking. Anna could hear her teeth clicking against the glass as she drank the wine.

'It's not the way it looks,' Carol said. 'I did everything I could to help him find you. He was desperate, looking for you.' She looked Anna in the eye and Anna could see she hated saying this. 'Maybe I'm wrong, and he just turned to me because he couldn't bear to be without you. I don't know. I don't think he does.'

Anna tried to smile at her. 'I don't know either,' she said. 'I don't know anything anymore. I'd expected everything could go back to normal, I really did, but everything's ruined.'

'We've got to talk about it,' Carol said.

'Please, I'd rather not.'

'No,' Carol said, 'not about that. About Tom. Your mother got up my nose and I told her I was going with Tom to shut her up.'

'You don't have to explain,' Anna said. 'I know what my mother's like.'

'No, listen,' Carol said, 'you've got to let me tell you. It's true, in a way . . . not that Tom's asked me to marry him, but we've been together and I love him. I *want* to marry him.'

Anna didn't know what to say so she said nothing while Carol continued to stare at nothing, looking miserable.

'Have you told Tom the way you feel?' Anna asked her. She had an idea Carol was not exactly making it up, but had taken some kindness of Tom's for love. Yes, Anna thought, he probably slept with her when he thought he'd lost me, that I'd run off with someone else. For the first time Anna saw that that was what Tom really might have thought.

'You don't understand,' Carol said, in a flat, sad voice.

For a moment, Anna wondered if there was something wrong with Carol mentally. 'Are you trying to tell me that Tom fell in love with you because he was worrying about me?' she asked. 'You don't honestly expect me to believe that?'

'It wasn't like that,' Carol said. She sounded desperate. 'He found

211

things out. You became a stranger to him. Or, at least, unreal.'

Anna didn't say anything: she understood too well.

'Oh, God,' Carol said. 'I'm so sorry. I'm so sorry what's happened to you.'

She raised her eyes and met Anna's. There was a long silence.

'Do you know what you've done?' Anna asked. 'All that time I was thinking that if I ever got free I'd come back to Tom. It was the only thing I had to hold on to. You've taken that away from me.'

God, she thought, I've begun to feel sorry for myself. I sound like a real victim.

It was something she really didn't want to be.

'Are you sure you really love him?' Carol was saying. 'You don't just want him to look after you while you lick your wounds?'

'Lick my wounds?' Anna said, incredulous.

'Yes,' Carol said. 'But what about him? Are you prepared to look after him while he gets over it?'

'Gets over what? Naturally I thought he'd be there for me now. And me for him. That's what love is.'

'You don't know what love is,' Carol said. 'You never did. If Tom still loves you and wants to be with you, I'd rather give him up than stand in his way. I want him to be happy. I'd rather he was happy with you, even if I think I'd die. Do you understand what that feels like?'

She started to cry. Anna tried to tell herself that Carol had always been able to weep, and the speech had probably come out of some novel or movie, an *old* novel or an *old* movie; they didn't have speeches like that today.

'Don't waste your tears,' Anna said. 'They won't work on me.' Christ, she thought, I sound just like my mother.

The doorbell rang. Carol wiped her wet face with her sleeve. She glanced at her watch. 'It's probably Tom,' she said. 'He had something important at the bank tonight.'

'I know he did,' Anna said. She felt like slapping Carol's face, the

212

way she was behaving as though she owned Tom. No wonder she'd always found it difficult keeping her boyfriends, she was so motherly.

'He had a lot of trouble at the bank because of you,' Carol said, 'after those newspaper stories.'

Anna remembered Tom's prim little boss. 'God,' she said, 'what a small-minded, miserable town this is.'

Carol, still sniffing, went to answer the door with the big towel still wrapped around her head.

Alone, Anna covered her face with her hands, breathing deeply to calm herself. Then she got up and went to the top of the stairs.

Tom had his arms round Carol. He was wearing evening dress. Looking down, Anna could see that he was going quite bald on the top of his head. It was the first time she'd ever been conscious that he was quite a lot older than she was.

He looked up and saw her. He put Carol away from him and ran up the stairs. 'I'm sorry, Anna,' he said. 'God, this is horrible.'

He was standing right next to her and he put out a hand to touch her but then took it back as if he was afraid of breaking her. Anna managed to laugh.

'Who'd have thunk it?' she said.

Carol came up the stairs and went by them without looking. She went into the sitting-room and sat down on the sofa. They followed. Carol still had a hurt look on her face and she still didn't look at them.

Then Anna saw Tom's face as he looked at Carol and she was afraid she was going to cry, and one crying woman in the room was enough. She saw all at once that Tom thought it was Carol he was betraying, not her. Anna couldn't compete, he'd never looked at her like that. But she knew, too, that Tom felt bound to her. He could not be anything but an honourable man. He wouldn't be able to let her down. If she still wanted him, he wouldn't be able to leave her.

'You've been crying,' Tom said to Carol.

'Don't worry, Tom, I haven't been beating her up,' Anna said.

213

Carol sniffed again but there weren't any tears. 'I'm sorry,' she said, 'I can't go on with this.' She turned to Anna. 'I never meant this to happen,' she said. 'I feel terrible. I'm terribly sorry for you, for what that terrible man must have done to you, but life goes on—'

'Sure,' Anna said, 'I know.' Her legs were trembling. 'Can I call a taxi, or can I get one outside?'

'Tom'll take you,' Carol said, making it sound as though she'd been married to Tom for years, and then she asked him, 'You haven't had too much to drink, have you?'

'Of course I'll take you,' Tom said. He fumbled in his pocket for his car keys. 'We've got to talk, Anna. I was going to tell you tomorrow.'

But in the car they had nothing to say. He only broke the silence when he stopped the car outside her house.

'I'm so sorry,' he said. 'I didn't know it was happening, and then it had happened and it was too late.'

'Don't kid me, Tom,' she said. 'You couldn't take the things you found out about me when my murky past came to light.'

She knew how he felt compelled to explain, as though he was turning down someone's bank loan.

'That murky past of mine,' she said, trying to tease him, pretending she didn't care. 'What did your mother say about my murky past?'

'I'll marry you, Anna, if that's what you want. I'll keep my word.'

'Don't be such an arsehole, Tom. What's the use of talking, we're all so fucking pathetic.'

'I don't want to abandon you if you really need me,' he said.

'Yes,' Anna said, 'it would look bad you dumping me in my hour of need. I've got to go in, Tom. I'm exhausted.' She opened the car door. 'And perhaps you should go and see if Carol's all right.'

Anna wasn't worried about Carol. She couldn't see Carol attempting anything desperate like pretending to commit suicide as a piece of emotional blackmail, not at least when Carol knew perfectly well that a woman who would do that wasn't the sort of wife a future bank

214

manager should have. 'You must have lots to tell her about your evening in Lombard Street, and what some jerk bank executive said to you and you said to him.'

Anna got out of the car and walked round to the driver's window. She intended to say, 'Tell Carol I hope you'll both be very happy,' but then she thought if she did, Carol might think she meant it and had forgiven her, and Anna hadn't.

So she walked away. The few yards between the pavement and her front door seemed to stretch for ever. She fumbled over the door key in her hurry to get inside. She closed the door behind her.

She stood in the hallway expecting him to ring the bell and tell her it was all a horrible mistake. Then she heard him drive away. 'I'm fine,' she said again, and she could hear how shaky her voice sounded. Why couldn't she tell him that the sores on her ankle hurt.

31

The next morning was Saturday. When Tom came into Carol's flat she saw the look on his face and she wanted to hug herself. He's chosen me, she thought, it's going to be all right. She ran across the room and put her arms round his neck. But she could see he was feeling bad about Anna and she took her arms away. Her guilt had melted away at the prospect of being with Tom, but now it returned, making her feel uncomfortable at the thought that Anna must be unhappy. She reached up to put her arms round Tom's neck again to show him she understood.

'Let's go and see her,' she said. 'Let's go there together tonight and ask her . . .' She didn't know what they should ask Anna.

'For permission?' Tom said. 'You want to ask her permission?'

'Yes,' Carol said, and she smiled at him. 'Something like that. Perhaps not quite so strong as permission.'

'Forgiveness?' he asked. He didn't seem too happy with that either.

But some hours later they left the flat together and got into Tom's car. They drove back towards Godlingford with no clear idea of what they were going to ask of Anna.

32

In the park Anna sat down on a bench near the pond to watch the ducks. She'd been walking aimlessly for hours and her feet were sore.

For some time she simply sat there, her mind a blank. She had no particular interest in ducks. Gradually, though, their goings-on attracted her attention. They were so magnificently absorbed in their own doings, so utterly parochial. It suited her mood, too, to see creatures so full of life and importance, so completely unaware of human concerns. Or rather, *her* concerns.

So she watched them. One of them, a lusty and splendidly burnished drake, seemed to her to have much in common with Tom. His nondescript little female quacked continuously with something between motherly solicitude and nagging: she was Carol. All the female ducks were like Carol. Anna could not identify herself with any one of them. There was one drab little grebe the others drove off from every crust of bread she tried to eat, but Anna could not identify with her. It struck her that many people around her would claim to recognize her in the victimized bird, but that was not in any way her perception of herself.

'If that makes it easier for them to deal with me, that's their problem,' she said.

She hadn't realized that she spoke aloud.

Then came a voice from close beside her. 'You'd almost think they were human, wouldn't you?'

Anna jumped as though the lusty drake had actually answered her back. She hadn't even noticed the elderly woman sitting on the bench beside her. The woman was very small, dressed in exotic purple and gold as though she was about to take the stage in a magic show. Her dark hair was cut in a straight bob. Anna was sure it was dyed, it had that particular matt tinge of chemical tinting. Her voice was beautiful, deep and sad, with a hint of a foreign accent. There was a powerful aura of drama about her; Anna could almost smell it.

'I'm sorry,' she said, 'I didn't realize you were there.' Actually, she wanted to hear the woman speak again.

'I don't mean to intrude,' the woman said. 'I think you want to be alone?'

It was a question. Anna had to say something. 'I've been alone all day,' she found herself saying, 'and it's done me no good at all.'

'If you like, tell me about it. It might help, to tell a stranger you will never see again.'

Anna looked at her and it was like a variation of the Ancient Mariner where she held her with her glittering eye and Anna had to tell her tale.

She told the stranger everything. The entire story, about Quimper and what he did to her, even down to the funnel he used on her; about Tom and Carol and how she had come home to find that everything she'd counted on was gone, and her life was destroyed. She told all this shamelessly. She ran the gamut from self-pity to blaming everyone who had ever been part of her life. It was a bravura performance of self-revelation she couldn't even have imagined she had in her. She felt she ought to be ashamed of such abandonment.

But when she'd finished, she felt incredibly relieved. This curious woman was right: she could only have spoken like that to a stranger. She was grateful and wondered how the woman had known how much she needed to let out everything she'd been bottling inside herself.

For a while the stranger said nothing. They both sat staring at the ducks. Then the older woman started to speak very slowly, as though she had to search for the words.

'There is nothing that I can say to you about what has happened to you, but if you will listen, I will tell you a little about myself.'

She turned on the bench and the folds of purple cloth fell back so that Anna could see her arm. The skin was horribly scarred.

Anna couldn't altogether hide her shock. The stranger pulled the cloth back quickly to cover herself. 'I suffered burns,' she said. 'They are unsightly, the scars, but so? At least I can put on my wig and wear sleeves and then I live a normal life. Others were not so lucky.' Her voice held no hint of bitterness or self-pity.

She went on and Anna listened, mesmerized by that lilting voice. 'I was a young girl in Hungary in 1956. My parents were involved in politics. The Russians came and the soldiers set fire to our house. My father was killed and my mother and brother disappeared. I was burned as you see. I lost everything. I was in an orphanage. Then a very remarkable woman brought me here to live in her house with other girls like me. It was near here. She ran a school for English girls and we Displaced Persons were educated with them. They called us DPs.'

The old woman sighed.

'Is that why you're here?' Anna asked her. 'As a reminder?'

'No,' she said. 'No, I came back here because while I lived in that wonderful woman's house, a man tried to rape me in this park, near here. I wanted to see it again.' She pointed towards tennis courts to the right.

Anna followed her finger. She couldn't imagine how a child could be raped in such a harmless-looking place. But no one could doubt that the woman was telling the truth. 'What happened?'

The old woman shrugged. 'He was a poor, sub-normal boy. He knocked me over and he had his thing out. I'd no idea a human penis

221

could be so *huge*. It was frightening, that.'

'What did you do?'

'In the end I succeeded in running away. I ran over there where the rhododendrons are close to the pond and I cleaned myself up and went back to the school.'

'Did they catch him? What did the police do?'

'You are the first person I have ever told. Once, I nearly told my husband, but when I started I looked at him, so strong and loving to me, and I wondered to myself if I was sure about what had happened. I even questioned if it had really happened at all, or if I had made it up. No, not made it up, but somehow *misread* what that sub-normal boy did.'

She paused, then went on, 'Do you know why I have told you this? It will sound odd to you now, perhaps, but one day you will understand. I tell you that I lost everything and that I was abused by another human being who did not even know me. I tell you because now I can say that those two things were *good* things for me.'

Anna must have looked as though she thought the woman had gone mad because her dark, distant expression softened into a smile. She put up her hand to stop Anna speaking.

'Oh, of course, I did not think that then. But when I lost everything, I learned from that woman who brought me here that it is not outside things that matter, it is the will to love that matters. I lost those I loved, but I learned that it is important to be open to love, not to hoard it. I still love my parents and my brother. Loss does not change that, but it must not be the end of love.

'And after I was raped, I knew that I could not escape from what happened to me by putting it on someone else – isn't that the phrase they use? No, I must take responsibility for myself. I have a wonderful life, and I believe that would not have been possible if I'd not had those experiences. I knew even then that I should not tell anyone what happened because then what that stupid young man did to me would take control of my life. I had the instinct to decide my life for myself.'

She looked at Anna and Anna felt that she was willing her to understand. 'I am not good at the words,' she said. 'What I am telling you is that most people, like your friends – your lover – live as though their lives are trains on railway tracks.' She laughed, and suddenly, as she threw her head back, she looked like a young girl again. 'When I lived here,' she said, almost shyly, 'the only thing I thought mattered about this place was the station. It is all station, isn't it? For the commuters to London. I used to think of the station as a great heart which pumped the people in every morning like blood and carried them away, and then, in the evening, brought them back polluted by life to be filtered and refreshed before they were sent back down the arteries to keep the great body of society going.'

Anna smiled at her. She could imagine her as she must have been then, small and fierce and independent.

'That was a young girl's fancy. What I want to tell you is that you have been given an opportunity. You might not like it, you might be angry that you should be singled out for no reason that you understand, but you have been. Don't fight it, use it. You will be happy, much happier than the other railway line people. But—'

She looked down at her hands, which were thin and brown, bent like a craftsman's tools. 'If you fail to understand this, if you try to be like the others, you will be very unhappy. You do not belong to that life any more, my child, you must go Beyond.'

It seemed to Anna that when this strange woman said 'beyond', it had to have a capital letter. The old woman asked, 'Do you see?'

Anna shook her head slowly, but not in denial of what the woman said, rather to clear her own mind.

'I know you have told me something important,' she said. 'I'm not sure that I understand yet, but I think I will. I'll try. But what you are saying is hard.'

'You must live the life you want to live. Are you sure that isn't what

223

has changed, that you have discovered the life you had isn't really what you want? It is a hard thing to face; it is very frightening because you have to jump into the dark.'

Anna thought she was scarcely listening to what the woman said, but as she spoke she suddenly felt excited. That was the first moment she thought she really knew what it felt like to be free. She was surprised. She thought she'd known since she got home, but this was something quite different. She actually had to grip the arm of the wooden bench or she felt she'd take off where she sat.

The woman gripped her arm. 'Here,' she said, 'take this. It's my card. I am Dr Kovac. I'm in town till next week. Then I leave to join my husband, who is an archeologist. His main interest was Egypt, but he wants now to go to a new dig in Mexico. Perhaps you can come with us?'

Anna was so startled that she had to stop herself telling Dr Kovac about the ten-day Golden Tour of Aztec Civilization. She stifled the unexpected urge. She'd always tended to fall back on old routines when in doubt, but she felt there was something symbolic about this moment and anyway it was a habit she'd got to break.

'But what use would I be?'

'You will Learn.' Again, the way Dr Kovac said the word, it had to have a capital letter. 'I decided to be a doctor while I was on a dig with my husband in Ethiopia. I qualified while he was working in Egypt. You will find your purpose also.'

'I've got to think,' Anna said.

'You're right,' Dr Kovac said. 'There will be plenty of people who try to take over your life because of what happened. They think they are helping, but they cannot help. Maybe I am one of them.'

She laughed as though she didn't really think so. Then she got up to go and Anna, too, got to her feet. She felt stiff. She towered over the little doctor.

Anna looked at the card the stranger had given her. 'Goodbye, Dr Kovac,' she said. 'Thank you.'

Quickly, almost embarrassed, Anna hugged her. Dr Kovac was the only person except Tom she had touched since she got home.

Anna walked home slowly and even when she'd shut the front door behind her, she was still distracted by the strange woman's hypnotic voice.

She listened to her messages on the answer-phone. There were several from her mother and two from a newspaper that wanted to interview her. There was another message from Godlingford Police; they'd received another call from France.

She turned the machine off. The police had tried to ring before. She supposed it would be about her car, the French would be wondering how long she would be leaving it there uncollected.

The house was quiet. Anna drew the heavy velvet curtains to shut out the night, and that deadened the sounds from the street, sounds of *Life* going on out there. Dr Kovac's capital letter syndrome was catching. It was creepy, the quiet. And she couldn't get over the feeling that someone was watching her. She felt as though she was back in Quimper's house and any moment the door might open and he'd walk in, all blue and bloated from being dead in the water. And, of course, it was true, people were watching her, naturally they were. She was a curiosity, for a little while at least. She told herself, they have to have something to look at when they aren't watching the telly.

She was glad of a respite, though, glad to be alone. But any small sound she made seemed to echo through the empty house. Her empty thoughts echoed in her empty head in her empty life. It sounded melodramatic. And why not? Why not be melodramatic?

And then she thought with a certain surprise, that she wasn't feeling sorry for herself, more irritated. Self-pity would've been easier, she could fill the void in her life with people who'd collude in her self-pity. That would be something other people could deal with. They'd know where they were with her. It was like a virus, she told herself, being a victim was like having a contagious disease, one victim infecting another.

225

Quimper, a monster from chaos, was himself a victim and a maker of victims. And Alain Dulac was her fault. If he'd never seen her in the window that poor man wouldn't have come to look for her. She tried to tell herself she didn't kill poor Alain Dulac. *I was only trying to help myself*, she thought, *what else could I have done? What else can victims do? It wasn't my fault the car broke down and the madman kidnapped me.*

The evening traffic outside in the street was heavy. She went to the desk at the far end of the room and got out a large brown envelope containing the newspaper cuttings about her capture and escape. Her mother had collected them for her. She knew that one day she'd want to read them.

She couldn't even get through the first of the newspapers. It was appalling. Where had they dredged up that terrible stuff? Who was this teenage girl, with her own name, who'd been the wildest, most promiscuous girl at school? Who on a school trip to Moscow had stripped off in Red Square and sold her Levi 501s to a passer-by? It was all so silly. No one could take it seriously. This girl had smoked marijuana. Well, she'd done that. Of course she had. She'd taken Es and danced all night. Naturally she had. Didn't the people who wrote these articles have teenage daughters? Yes, they might have them, but they ignored what they knew when they wrote titillation for the prurient hypocrites out there to read.

Anna put the cutting aside. She noticed a photo of Tom. Underneath was the caption: 'Torment of Trusting Tom'. He had his arm raised to shield his face from the photographer. This was worse, this was serious. The article about Tom was headlined: MY DREAM GIRL BECAME A NIGHTMARE. And where had they got hold of that photo of her at sixteen dressed up like a punk? Her mother. Her mother must've given it to the paper, or sold it. How could she? Anna's sixteen-year-old face, looking like a mask with dark sockets for eyes, black lipstick, stared up at her.

226

Perhaps one day looking at that silly photo would be fun, but in the newspaper's story it was implied that a girl like that was bound to get herself murdered or raped. People who didn't know her would agree. And her friends? Even if they didn't accept this grotesque newspaper version of who she was, they would start from there when they defended her. She could hear them, friends like Nick, saying, 'She's not at all the way the newspapers have made her out to be . . .' Or others who were not her friends, saying, 'I can't believe she could have fooled everybody.' That bitch of a secretary of Nick's, Jill, she'd say that. Flowers or not, Anna thought, Jill was a bitch.

She began to sort through the cuttings. She picked out a Sunday tabloid interview with her mother, the Victim Mum. She felt sick. Her mother was no victim, why should she want to make herself out to be one? Or perhaps she was, in her own way. She'd started out as a real stereotype victim, unmarried, pregnant, shocked parents banishing her from the house. Yes, she had been a victim, but she'd learned to use it to her advantage. Anna tried to imagine her mother talking to her like Dr Kovac had. It was so unlikely the idea made her smile. Then she thought, even if she had, I wouldn't have listened.

All this had been so much part of her childhood, her mother whining about everybody else, everything and everyone being unfair to her. Anna had taken it for granted. Now it was her turn, and she could pass it on, this victim status, as her mother had tried to do to her. Even now she could make Tom leave Carol and do his duty by her, although he loved Carol. And Carol felt so guilty because she had fallen in love with him that she'd let him go. Even Nick wouldn't fire her, although keeping her on was like having someone outside the shop with a megaphone shouting 'Don't go, stay at home'.

It would be pretty easy to lie back and let it happen. No one could blame her, they wouldn't dare.

But then she thought, I wasn't really a victim, was I? I killed Quimper. I wonder how it would be if I told Inspector Baubel that

227

when I go to France to collect my car? What would happen if I tell my mother's newspaper a story about hitting Quimper with the fence post, about how good it was seeing him dead.

Her head ached. She was about to put the cuttings aside when she heard something. The sound came from the kitchen.

She held her breath, telling herself it was a mouse, the house was old, it had mice. She often thought she should get a cat.

But no, it was something much bigger than a mouse. There was somebody in the kitchen. Call the police, she told herself, and don't make a sound. People got killed when they disturbed intruders. Then she thought, don't call the police, think of the headlines, deal with it the best you can. Run out, run to the neighbours.

But instead she picked up a poker from the fireplace. Moving slowly along the hallway, keeping close to the wall, she went to the kitchen. There was a light that shouldn't have been there under the door and she could hear the intruder moving about. She stopped. It was absurd, but it sounded as though he was making himself something to eat.

She pushed the door wide open and, without giving herself time to think, shouted 'Hands up' and jabbed the point of the poker against the base of the skull of the man making himself at home at her kitchen sink.

When he turned round to face her she dropped the poker.

'Anna,' Toto said, and came out with a stream of incoherent French.

'What are you doing here?' she shouted at him in English. She couldn't think of the French words. She couldn't think of anything. It was like seeing an apparition. She was outraged that he had forced his way into her life. Then she took several deep breaths. Quimper wasn't there. This was Toto. She was safe in her own house in her own country. She was able to speak French again.

'How did you get into my house?' she asked.

He turned and pointed to the back door. 'I picked the lock.' He had an idiot matter-of-factness over this accomplishment.

228

'But what are you doing here? How did you get here?'

He looked sly. 'I didn't know what to do.'

She stood and watched him eating. If she tried to make him go, he might lose his temper the way he often did when he was crossed. She'd seen the way he was. She'd never felt much fear of him before but she was afraid now, in her own kitchen, in her own home, in her own town. Toto was frightening in such familiar surroundings.

'Why didn't you stay with your fishermen friends?' she asked.

Toto looked blank. 'I went home, but Quimper wasn't there. The police were there.'

'Yes,' she said, 'but why come here?'

'Godlingford,' Toto said.

He was backward, a sad case. She'd told him that make-believe to distract herself, not really to entertain him, but he'd taken her fantasy Godlingford to be real. It was sad, but she was impatient.

'But why didn't you go back to your friends on the coast? They'd have looked after you.'

Toto hung his head, looking up at her under his pale eyelashes. 'Joseph told me to go,' he said. 'He said to lie low.'

'Lie low? Why?'

'I hurt a man,' Toto said. 'With this.' He pulled a long-bladed knife from his belt. 'I stuck it in him,' he said.

He used a Breton dialect word which she didn't understand, so she wasn't certain whether he'd killed or simply wounded the man. He is dangerous, she thought, really dangerous.

'OK, Toto,' she said, 'put it away.'

He put the knife on the kitchen table, then he took a catapult out of his pocket, followed by a length of wire like one she remembered seeing Quimper take with him when he went to snare rabbits. These country weapons looked out of place on her kitchen table.

'You can't stay here,' she said. 'You'll have to go.'

She began to back towards the door. She felt behind her for the door handle, then she fumbled for the key. It wasn't on the inside. If she could get out and slam the door on him, she could lock him inside and perhaps have time to call the police before he broke the door down. But he was too quick for her. He pinned her against the wall. The knife was in his hand again. The point of it pricked the skin under her ear.

'Don't be silly,' she said. There was always the chance he was only playing a game. Her voice sounded odd, thin and weak. 'In the other room we can sit down and talk. Tell me how you found me? How did you get across to England?' She stopped talking. What am I going to do now? she thought.

He was suspicious. 'You hid from me? Why are you hiding from me?'

'I wasn't hiding from you,' she said, 'this is where I live. After Quimper died . . .'

Toto looked unhappy. 'Did the police kill him?' he asked. The way he said police was full of menace, as though if she said they'd had a hand in Quimper's death he would plunge out of the house into the street and find a policeman to kill.

'No,' she said, 'it was an accident. He fell . . .'

'No,' Toto said. 'You're lying. He didn't fall; he wouldn't fall.' There were tears in his eyes. In spite of everything, he'd loved Quimper. She was surprised.

'The police found his body,' she said.

Suddenly he jumped on her, knocking her to the floor, holding her by the throat. She tried to push him away but she couldn't.

'I didn't kill him,' she said. The words barely came out.

But he heard. He loosened his grip on her throat and pulled her up to a semi-sitting position, slumped against the arm of a chair. She saw his forehead contort with the effort of understanding what she'd said, and then, slowly, a look of horror swept across his face as though her words had triggered a thought that it hadn't occurred to him to think before.

'You did it,' he said. 'You killed him, you did, didn't you? You tricked

230

him the way you tricked me to let you loose and then you killed him.'

'No,' she said. 'It's not true. He fell into the quarry. He'd been drinking.'

'He never fell,' Toto said.

'I'll prove it,' she said. 'He fell.'

Toto looked puzzled, but he didn't try to stop her going into the living-room. He followed close behind her. She could smell the foul stink of his sweat, days and days of old sweat. It brought back the house in Brittany, but then it hadn't ever gone away.

She picked up the newspaper cuttings on the floor. Toto, looking sulky, stood over her.

He couldn't read English. She didn't think he could read his own language.

'I'll read it for you.'

Toto nodded. He had a child-like respect for the mysteries of print. She read him a report of her rescue, of how they had found her.

'You can see I was chained,' she said. 'How can I have killed Quimper if I was chained?'

'You tricked him and then hit him over the head,' Toto said.

'No,' she said, 'he wasn't in the kitchen. He was dead at the quarry.'

Toto took the newspaper from her. He stared at it as though it meant something to him. 'The quarry?' he said.

'Yes. And how could I kill him? It was an accident. He was drunk and he fell.'

She saw that he wanted to believe her. She waited while his slow mind worked. She was frightened and felt she hadn't convinced him, that he knew by some animal instinct that she'd killed Quimper. The police had accepted the evidence that she couldn't have done it, but Toto seemed to know she was lying.

The telephone rang in the hall. Toto took out his knife, looking round to see where the noise came from. She smiled and picked up the phone, trying to seem calm.

231

It was Inspector Parrish.

Toto stood at her shoulder, putting his ear forward to hear the voice in the instrument although he couldn't understand the language. His breath was foul. He had stunk in Brittany but so had she. Now it was difficult to breathe with him so close.

Inspector Parrish sounded hesitant. 'Sorry to disturb you so late, but I tried earlier,' he said. 'I don't want to alarm you unduly, but we've had reports from the French police . . . well, what it comes down to is that there's just a chance the young man, Toto, who lived with the man Quimper in France, may be trying to reach you.'

Toto didn't recognize his name or Quimper's in Inspector Parrish's English, but he was agitated. He tried to take the receiver from her. She turned, keeping it beyond his reach.

'What are you saying?' Toto asked. 'Why are you speaking like that?' He couldn't understand why she was speaking another language when he had only really heard her speak French before.

'Yes,' she said to Inspector Parrish, trying to keep her voice unconcerned, as though she were talking to a casual acquaintance, 'he's here now.'

'You mean he's in the house with you?' Inspector Parrish said.

Anna could tell he was also trying to keep any sense of alarm out of his voice.

She forced herself to sound calm. 'Yes,' she said.

'I have to tell you he's wanted by the French police for killing a man. Is he armed?'

'Yes,' Anna said, and her voice trembled. So Toto had killed a man. He was truly dangerous. She hadn't believed it. She wasn't safe. 'He's got—' And then the phone went dead.

33

Mrs Turl tried to telephone. The line was still engaged. She had tried several times already.

She told herself that she'd better go to see Anna. She didn't want there to be bad feeling between them. She changed into the most severe outfit in her wardrobe, a blue suit with a tailored jacket with a narrow, flattering waist. She thought this made her look like a concerned but sophisticated mother, very much like her own mother, who now lived in a home on the south coast near Eastbourne.

Sophie Turl considered getting the car out and driving to Anna's, but thought better of it. She felt the need to lend an aura of urgency to her mission of mercy. She rang for a taxi and prepared to be taken to her daughter in her hour of need.

The taxi was stopped as the driver tried to turn into Anna's street. A policeman stepped forward and spoke to the driver.

'What is it? What's going on?' Mrs Turl said. Her voice was shrill with frustration. The police had blocked the road.

'Make up your mind, lady,' the driver told her. 'I'm off. This is costing me money.'

Mrs Turl got out of the taxi. She walked up the street before the policeman could stop her.

Outside Anna's house, Inspector Parrish and Sergeant Dicks were concealed behind a privet hedge. The sergeant stepped out and grabbed Mrs Turl by the arm.

'Let go of me,' she said. She intended to shout, but the sight of the policeman stifled the cry and her words sounded like a hiss.

'You shouldn't be here, madam. Get out of here,' Sergeant Dicks said.

'But my daughter lives here. I want to see my daughter.'

'Get her out of here,' Inspector Parrish ordered.

Mrs Turl would have protested further, but she found herself borne away by two burly policeman. When she opened her mouth to scream, one of them put his hand firmly over her face.

As she was half-carried back down the pavement she saw that there were men lying low behind the parked cars in the street.

'That was a close call,' Sergeant Dicks said.

'Bloody women,' Inspector Parrish said.

He hated waiting. He thought he had covered every detail, but when he had time to think, he began to doubt. Men were at the back of the house as well. They called him and asked if he wanted them to enter the house through the rear. They were eager but Inspector Parrish told them to wait. He could see Anna Turl and the Frenchman through the glass panels of the front door, silhouetted against the light in the hall.

'He's a nasty-looking bastard,' Sergeant Dicks whispered to his boss.

'Well,' Inspector Parrish said, 'he would be, wouldn't he?'

'I could take a shot at him,' Dicks said.

Inspector Parrish shook his head. Sergeant Dicks was keen to use the rifle but the inspector didn't want any gunfire, not unless it was absolutely necessary. Besides, Anna and the Frenchman were talking. He could see them quite clearly talking.

'It'd be a clean shot,' Dicks said.

Before Inspector Parrish could answer, the two figures in the house started moving.

'Something's up,' Dicks said.

234

They could hear the man screaming. He was in a rage.

'Shall I shoot?' Dicks asked.

Inspector Parrish couldn't help smiling that Dicks was so keen to shoot someone.

'No,' he said, 'not yet.'

They could hear Anna Turl talking loudly.

'You must go,' she said.

Toto's cursing and screaming stopped. They could tell Anna was trying to speak in a normal voice, trying to soothe the Frenchman. They strained to listen, but couldn't make out more than the odd word and that was in a foreign language. 'Go now,' she was saying, 'stay in the park by the lake. Tomorrow morning I'll come to you there.'

Toto loomed through the glass behind the door.

He opened the door and was about to step out when Anna Turl stopped him. It was as though she realized why it was so quiet outside.

'No,' she shouted. 'Toto, come back,' she called out to him in English.

But he was gone, closing the Yale lock on the door behind him.

'You are surrounded,' Inspector Parrish called to Toto. 'Put down your weapon.'

Beside him Sergeant Dicks took careful aim.

On the steps outside Anna Turl's front door, Toto was blinded by lights. He heard a man shouting in a strange language. He didn't know what the man was saying. He heard Anna call in French from inside the house. 'Throw down your knife,' she said. 'They want you to drop your weapons.'

'What's she saying?' Sergeant Dicks asked. He was very excited.

'I don't know, but don't shoot,' Parrish said.

Toto was reaching inside his coat when Sergeant Dicks fired. Three times he fired. One of the shots shattered the glass panel in the front door.

There was a long silence.

235

'He was going for a gun,' Sergeant Dicks said as he and Inspector Parrish approached Toto's body.

Inspector Parrish felt for a pulse. The man was dead. Inspector Parrish pointed to what the Frenchman had been reaching for. 'A sling shot,' he said. 'that's what he was going for, not a gun.'

He took the catapult from Toto's hand.

'How was I to know?' Sergeant Dicks asked.

'Calm down,' Inspector Parrish said. It was too late for recriminations. He stepped over the body and went into the house to see if the woman was all right.

34

A police constable stopped Tom's car as he tried to turn into Willow Walk, Anna's street.

'Sorry, sir,' the constable said, 'we've had to close this street.'

'But—' Tom said.

'What's going on?' Carol asked, leaning across Tom to speak to the constable.

'There's been an incident in the street,' the policeman said. 'An armed incident. It's all over bar the shouting.'

Tom and Carol got out of the car and walked up to the fluttering tape the police had placed across the road. There was a crowd of people who lived in the street. They were complaining that they wanted to go home and the police kept telling them to go down the road to the Birch Lane Primary School, where they would be accommodated until the siege was over.

Tom and Carol looked for Anna among the crowd.

'She's probably safe at that school,' Tom said, 'or she may have gone out and know nothing about it.'

Carol put her hand on his arm. 'Look,' she said, 'there's Anna's mother.' Carol looked again. 'That is her, isn't it?' she said. 'She looks different.'

Tom followed her gaze and saw Mrs Turl at the very front of the crowd.

She was talking excitedly to a young woman holding a microphone.

'My God,' Tom said, 'she's the last person I want to see.'

Carol wondered why the woman with the microphone was talking to Mrs Turl. She felt a nervous flutter in her stomach. Please God, she prayed silently, let her be alive, don't let her have killed herself.

Then there was a stirring in the crowd and everyone fell silent. Anna came out of her house with Inspector Parrish. She walked beside him to a police car at the kerb. She marched down the path to the pavement without looking to left or right. She showed no interest at all in the silent bystanders. She and Inspector Parrish might have been leaving to go out to dinner together.

Tom pushed to the front of the crowd.

'Anna,' he shouted, 'Anna, are you all right?'

Anna seemed not to hear him. She got into the car with Inspector Parrish.

'It's your fiancé,' Parrish said to her, recognizing Tom. 'Do you want to talk to him?'

'No,' Anna said, 'I don't want to talk to him.'

She didn't look at Tom or Carol as the car moved slowly past them.

'Is there someone we can contact for you?' Inspector Parrish asked. He was puzzled at how cool she was.

'No,' Anna said, 'I don't want anybody.'

'What was Toto shouting?' Inspector Parrish asked. 'My French wasn't up to translating.'

Inspector Parrish thought the girl was odd. Now she said what he thought was a very strange thing.

'Poor Toto,' she said. 'He was a victim from the start.'

Inspector Parrish didn't know what to say. Then he caught sight of Mrs Turl pressing forward against the car. 'There's your mother,' he said. 'I suppose you'll want to see her.'

He wished he could ignore Mrs Turl. He didn't relish the thought of her company in the car.

'You suppose wrong,' Anna said. 'I don't want to see her.'

Mrs Turl's face was at the car window. Inspector Parrish turned to look at Anna sitting beside him. He thought, she hasn't got the sort of look on her face she should have. Inspector Parrish saw a lot of victims of crime, every day he saw them and she didn't look like one of them. She looked excited, almost triumphant. And then he thought, no, not exactly triumphant, it's as though she's got *conviction*, like one of those born-again people.

'Anna,' Mrs Turl shouted. She banged on the car window, but Anna didn't turn her head.

'Let's go,' Anna said to the driver, 'come on, let's get out of here.'

The car accelerated and Mrs Turl's outraged face fell away.

Inspector Parrish turned to look at the crowd but he saw that Anna was still looking straight ahead.

'What are you going to do now?' Inspector Parrish asked, making conversation. He expected her to say she was looking forward to settling down after everything that had happened.

'I'm going to Mexico,' she said.

'Oh,' he said, 'a nice holiday then? Much the best thing to get away for a while. Everything will have died down when you come home and you'll be able to get back to normal.'

She said something. The noise from the crowd drowned her voice and he couldn't hear her properly. They sat in silence as the car passed through the crowd. Then Inspector Parrish realized what it was Anna said she planned to do. She'd said she was going to go Beyond. She made it sound as though Beyond was a real place. It struck Inspector Parrish as an odd way to talk about a holiday, but when he looked at her face he didn't like to ask her what she meant.

Then she turned to him. She said in a loud, clear voice with the ring of exhilaration, so that he could not mistake what she said.

'I'm going to be happy,' she said, 'and now I know how, I can't wait to start.'

239